"I'll watch Samson for you."

Wyatt's hand paused and, hallelujah, he stopped writing. "What?"

"I'll watch Samson so you can attend your meeting with the mayor."

"Don't you have appointments, Dr. Evans?"

"I just finished up with my last patient right before you and Prissy arrived." She nuzzled the alpaca's neck, then flashed Wyatt a soothing smile. "I'm absolutely free and clear the rest of the afternoon."

"What's the catch?"

The man was too perceptive. "I'm offended you would even ask."

"What's the catch, Remy?"

"Okay, okay. You turn that ticket into a warning, forget about the fine and I'll help you out with your nephew."

"Bribing an officer of the law?"

"You say *bribe*. I say *negotiate*. So? What do you say?"

Wyatt gaped at her for three full seconds, looking slightly appalled they were even having this conversation. But he wasn't saying no, either.

Remy pushed her advantage. "Tick tock, my friend." She tapped her wrist with her index finger. "Yes or no? Do we have a deal or not?"

Renee Ryan grew up in a Florida beach town where she learned to surf, sort of. With a degree from FSU, she explored career opportunities at a Florida theme park and a modeling agency and even taught high school economics. She currently lives with her husband in Wisconsin, and many have mistaken their overweight cat for a small bear. You may contact Renee at reneeryan.com, on Facebook or on Twitter, @reneeryanbooks.

Books by Renee Ryan

Love Inspired

Thunder Ridge

Surprise Christmas Family
The Sheriff's Promise

Village Green

Claiming the Doctor's Heart
The Doctor's Christmas Wish

Love Inspired Historical

Charity House

The Marshal Takes a Bride
Hannah's Beau
Loving Bella
The Lawman Claims His Bride
Charity House Courtship
The Outlaw's Redemption
Finally a Bride

Visit the Author Profile page at Harlequin.com for more titles.

The Sheriff's Promise

Renee Ryan

LOVE INSPIRED

INSPIRATIONAL ROMANCE

LOVE INSPIRED®

INSPIRATIONAL ROMANCE

Recycling programs
for this product may
not exist in your area.

ISBN-13: 978-1-335-48887-9

The Sheriff's Promise

This edition published by arrangement with Harlequin Books S.A.

For questions and comments about the quality of this book, please contact us at CustomerService@Harlequin.com.

Love Inspired
22 Adelaide St. West, 40th Floor
Toronto, Ontario M5H 4E3, Canada
www.Harlequin.com

Printed in U.S.A.

Two are better than one; because they have
a good reward for their labour.
—*Ecclesiastes* 4:9

For Donnell,
who walked with me every step of the way
and always answered the phone
when I needed to be talked off the ledge.
You are, quite simply, the best of the best!

Chapter One

Sheriff Wyatt Holcomb booted up his computer. Adrenaline still hummed in his veins. The traffic accident he'd just left had included injuries, one of them a little boy around his nephew's age. He'd done what he could. The rest was in the hands of the ER doctors.

Wyatt pushed the incident out of his head. He had less than two hours to prepare for his meeting with the newly elected mayor, also his boss now that Thunder Ridge was a consolidated city-county. The budget review would determine whether she signed off on his request to hire another deputy.

Wyatt really needed that deputy.

Thunder Ridge might be on the smaller side, with a population of 15,128. But it was also a resort town in the Colorado Rocky Mountains, which skewed those numbers during the high seasons. And never in Wyatt's favor. A qualified law enforcement officer would ease the department's workload and allow him to focus his own efforts more efficiently. Both at work and at home, neither of which were currently receiving his best.

Drumming his fingers on the desk, he smiled as the wallpaper on his computer popped into view. The picture of his seven-year-old nephew mugging for the camera never failed to lift his spirits. He loved Samson with the heart of a father, which he'd become temporarily thanks to his sister's bad choices.

Wyatt's smile faded. Ever since he'd assumed custody, he'd been pulled in too many directions and was possibly— probably—teetering on the edge of burnout. He could feel the mental exhaustion creeping in at moments like this, when he had too many tasks left in the day and not enough hours to complete them.

Determined to do better, he focused on what he could control and clicked open the correct spreadsheet. Methodically—Wyatt was nothing if not methodical—he began a detailed review of his proposed budget, looking for places where he could cut expenses. He was on the seventh line item when he caught a movement in his peripheral vision coming from outside his office window.

He did a fast double take just as something brown and furry ducked out of sight.

Something with straight, pointy ears.

Something that wore a bright pink bridle.

It was that splash of pink-on-brown that had Wyatt surging to his feet. *Not again.*

He'd barely rounded his desk when the animal reappeared in the window and looked straight at him, long-lashed beady eyes and all. Their gazes held a split second and, if Wyatt wasn't mistaken, the pink-bedazzled alpaca actually winked at him.

His temper kicked into overdrive.

Eyes still focused on the furry menace, he put two fingers at his temples and rubbed, hard. The animal chose that moment to wander out of his line of vision. *Oh, no, you don't.*

Wyatt immediately headed for the exit.

"Hey, Sheriff," his administrative assistant called out as he passed her desk. "Where're you going in such a hurry?"

"No time to explain, Doris." He gave a quick wave over his head to the middle-aged keeper of his schedule, self-proclaimed departmental mother hen and all-around organizational marvel. "Back in thirty."

"Yeah, well, you better make that twenty. If you're late for your meeting with the mayor, you can kiss that new deputy goodbye."

"I won't be late," he shouted over his shoulder.

Apparently unconvinced, Doris continued, "You blow this, Sheriff, and I will personally—"

Wyatt shut the door on the rest of her threat. He'd heard it all before. And didn't disagree. He had no plans of losing the ongoing budget war with the mayor.

Nor did he plan to lose the battle of law and order on his streets.

Once outside, he looked left, then right. Then…there. Up ahead, he caught the woolly hips rounding the corner of Main Street. The animal could move when she put her mind to it. Normally, Prissy sauntered along as if her world were made of rainbows and gumdrops.

Wyatt took off at a dead run.

He'd nearly caught up with the animal when Mrs. Brooks, owner of the Latte Da Diner, cut him off at the pass. "About time you showed up." She jammed two fists on her sizable hips. "Remy's llama is eating my geraniums. The ones I planted in my new window boxes just this morning."

Wyatt opened his mouth to speak, but now that Mrs. Brooks had begun her rant, there was no stopping her. She had many nice things to say about the *llama's* owner, Dr. Remy Evans, one of two female veterinarians in town. But that didn't mean the diner owner had any use for Remy's animal. Not with that *llama's* head currently buried in her geraniums.

When the woman finally paused to draw a breath, Wyatt said the first thing that came to mind. "Prissy is not a llama. She's an alpaca."

His desperate attempt to calm the diner owner seemed to work. She blinked several times, then asked, "What's the difference?"

"Alpacas are several hundred pounds lighter than llamas," Wyatt said. "They have smaller faces, shorter noses, and they can, so I've been told, learn tricks."

Tricks, like escaping their pens and making a general nuisance of themselves on Wyatt's streets. Several times this week, to be exact.

No more, he promised himself. No more ignored warnings. No more allowing a beautiful veterinarian to sweet-talk him out of a citation. This time, Remy had earned herself a hefty fine. But first...

Wyatt pushed up his sleeves and approached the animal. "Prissy, stop eating Mrs. Brooks's flowers."

The alpaca's face remained buried in the window box. Thus proving herself as ornery as her owner. Why wasn't he surprised?

Wyatt whistled once, low and through his teeth. At last, trouble on four legs lifted her bushy head. The animal had a mouthful of bright pink geraniums that weirdly matched her bridle. Figured Remy's alpaca would color-coordinate her valiant attempt at ruining his day.

"I don't get paid enough for this job," he muttered under his breath.

"What's that, Sheriff?"

"Nothing, Mrs. Brooks." Wyatt gripped the alpaca's bridle under her chin, then jerked his own chin toward the massacred flower box. "I'll see that Dr. Evans reimburses you for the damage."

"I'm sure she will. She's a good girl, that one. I've always liked her. Almost as much as her older sister, Quinn. Remy is such a sweet, personable girl. And pretty. She's become my new favorite vet in town since she came home."

Right now, Wyatt had other names for the woman's favorite animal doctor, none of which he cared to voice. Holding his silence, he steered the alpaca away from the Latte Da. A block from their destination, he dug out his cell phone and sent Remy a quick text. I have something that belongs to you. Meet me behind the clinic in two minutes.

Wyatt secured the phone back in its case on his belt, then reached for the alpaca's bridle once again. "Come on, Prissy. Let's get you back to your owner."

As casually as if this was just another day on planet Earth, the alpaca followed along at Wyatt's clipped pace. She took a few prancing steps when she saw Remy's veterinary clinic up ahead. The area behind the building was empty. No Remy. No vet tech.

Wyatt tied Prissy to a bike rack, pulled out his phone and sent another text. Outside. Now.

Trouble on two legs exited the building, blue eyes flashing, shiny black hair tied back in a ponytail and swinging wildly, her willowy yet curvy body hidden beneath a white lab coat. "All right, *Sheriff*. What's so urgent that couldn't—?" Her feet ground to a halt. "What are you doing with my alpaca?"

"Returning her to her rightful owner, after she decided to roam the streets of Thunder Ridge."

Remy's gaze bounced from Wyatt to the alpaca, then back to Wyatt. "Prissy got out of her pen again?"

He held Remy's gaze. "Evidently."

"I don't see how."

"Don't you?"

The question earned him a frown. "She's usually so obedient."

Wyatt felt the muscle in his jaw tick. The woman actually sounded stunned. He pulled out the ticket book from his back pocket, flipped open the cover and said, "Maybe a citation will clear up your confusion."

"You don't need to write me a ticket. I'll fix the pen."

Wyatt had heard that one before. At least two other times this week. "I'm giving you a citation, Remy. As an added bonus for taking up my valuable time and costing taxpayers money, I'm slapping you with a five-hundred-dollar fine."

"You can't do that."

"Watch me." He continued filling in the blanks with his trusty pen. "You're also going to pay for the damage Prissy did to Mrs. Brooks's flower boxes."

"Oh, well. Okay. I suppose that's…fair."

"You *suppose*?"

"You don't have to be sarcastic, Wyatt."

Her use of his first name spoke of their long history, a history he'd rather forget. Not that Remy ever brought it up, either.

Better that way.

Picking up on the tension between the town sheriff and her owner, Prissy shifted from one foot to the other. Wyatt reached out to steady the animal. Remy also shot out her hand, her fingers grazing across his. As if burned, they both snapped their hands back.

The alpaca, now highly agitated, shifted closer to her owner and rewarded Wyatt for his troubles by spitting on his shirt.

Torn between amusement and horror, Remy placed her hand on the alpaca's neck and attempted to diffuse the situation with some good old-fashioned deflection. "Relax, Prissy. The big bad scary sheriff didn't mean to frighten you. No, he didn't." Remy cooed the words as she stroked the soft fleece. "He's very sorry. Aren't you, Sheriff? Aren't you sorry?"

Wyatt met her eyes, and—*oh, boy*—that was one unhappy, not-sorry lawman. "She spit on me."

It took heroic effort for Remy not to stare at the wet spot, while simultaneously pretending she wasn't aware of every leanly muscled inch of irritated six-foot-three male. "It's your own fault, Wyatt. Prissy has a delicate disposition. She spits when she's stressed. You should know this by now."

He made a face. "I have an important meeting with the mayor this afternoon, which I cannot attend wearing alpaca spit across my chest."

Remy frowned. "How, exactly, is that my problem?"

"How, exactly, is it not?"

Sighing, Remy looked away from those dark, penetrating eyes that were currently hard as granite. She knew from experience that those same eyes could soften to a compelling light amber when Wyatt was amused or having fun.

At the moment, he was neither.

"Look," she said, putting what she hoped was a large dose of humility in her voice. "I'm sorry about your shirt. All I can do is apologize and make restitution and—"

"You could also do a better job securing your pens."

A valid point. Out of bluster and witty comebacks, Remy attempted a different approach. "Come on, Wyatt. Cut me a break, just this once."

He barked out an emphatic "No," then returned his attention to his ticket book and began writing furiously. The man seemed to be in an awful big hurry.

He also seemed highly motivated.

Remy tried not to panic. No way could she afford a $500 fine and still meet the bank's deadline for the down payment on her loan request. No down payment, no loan. No loan, and Remy would miss her opportunity to purchase the private zoo next to her ranch.

What to do?

Deflection hadn't worked. Her attempt at humor had fallen flat. Perhaps it was time to admit defeat. "I know you're angry, and rightfully so. But there must be something I can do to convince you not to—"

He lifted a finger. "Stop talking. I mean it, Remy. Not another word."

She was about to give him what-for when he pulled out his cell phone to answer an incoming call. "This is Sheriff Holcomb."

Well, okay, then. He hadn't meant to be offensive.

A one-sided conversation ensued, with the person on the other end doing all the talking and Wyatt doing all the listening. While pretending grave interest in Prissy's bridle, Remy studied the man out of the corner of her eye. Two years older than her, Wyatt had been the star of her girlish, teenage dreams. Until he'd crushed them one day with four horrible words. "You're not my type."

That had been seventeen years ago. Entirely too long for Remy to hold a grudge, which, of course, she didn't. That would make her petty and immature. She was neither.

Wyatt sighed heavily into the cell phone, dragging her back to the here and now. Another few seconds passed. Then he ran a hand through his hair, leaving the short, dark chestnut strands sticking straight up. It was at that point Remy realized Wyatt wasn't wearing his hat, or his mirrored sunglasses.

"Got it. Be right there." He disconnected the call.

The conversation had clearly upset him. But it was his stricken expression that had her asking, "What's wrong? What's happened?"

"That was Samson's teacher at the day care that runs his after-school program." He shook his head in utter bafflement. "He's been suspended for the rest of the day."

"That's terrible." But not wholly unexpected. Remy may have been back home for only six months, but even she knew the boy had a gift for finding trouble. "What did he do this time?"

"I'm not really sure. Something about demo days, dissatisfaction with unnecessary walls and...blueprints?"

"That doesn't make any sense."

"No, it doesn't." Wyatt rolled his shoulders. "But this is his second strike. One more and he's out for good."

Remy gasped. "They wouldn't expel a seven-year-old boy, would they?"

"That will completely depend on Samson."

"Poor kid." Remy really liked the little boy. Sure, Samson was rambunctious, but that was because he missed his mother. Understandable, under the circumstances. And, yeah, maybe the boy was a bit hard to handle at times. What kid wasn't? So what if the seven-year-old had a fondness for relocating lizards and frogs into little girls' backpacks? Remy admired the boy's creativity. In fact, Samson kind of reminded Remy of herself at his age.

And just like that, a solution popped into her head. "Wyatt, didn't you mention an important meeting this afternoon with the mayor?"

"I did, yes."

"Soooo... That means this incident with Samson puts you in something of a bind?"

"Doris will watch him."

Remy knew Wyatt's administrative assistant very well.

The woman was scary with a capital *S*. She ran the sheriff's office with a no-nonsense, by-the-book commitment to order that would put an army general to shame. "Doesn't Doris have other, more pressing duties than babysitting your nephew?"

"She'll understand, this one time." Wyatt gave a single head bob as if to convince himself as much as Remy, then flipped open the ticket book. "Now, where were we?"

Oh, no. "You were about to say you're on a time crunch."

Another nod. But no eye contact. Just more scribbling.

Fortifying herself with a quick breath, Remy blurted out, "I'll watch Samson for you."

Wyatt's hand paused and stopped writing, and he lifted his head. "What?"

"I'll watch Samson so you can attend your meeting with the mayor."

"Don't you have appointments—" he looked pointedly at the nameplate on her lab coat "—Dr. Evans?"

"I just finished up with my last patient right before you and Prissy arrived." She nuzzled the alpaca's neck, then flashed Wyatt with the soothing smile she reserved for her most anxious pet owners. "I'm absolutely free and clear the rest of the afternoon."

"What's the catch?"

The man was too perceptive. "I'm offended you would even ask."

"What's the catch, Remy?"

"Okay, okay. You turn that ticket into a warning, forget about the fine, and I'll help you out with your nephew."

"Bribing an officer of the law?"

She brushed away the question with a quick flick of her wrist. "You say *bribe*. I say *negotiate*. So? What do you say? Am I hanging out with your nephew this afternoon and thereby saving the day?"

Wyatt gaped at her for three full seconds, looking slightly appalled they were even having this conversation. But she noticed he wasn't saying no, either.

Remy pushed her advantage. "Tick tock, my friend." She tapped her wrist with her index finger. "Yes or no? Do we have a deal or not?"

"I can't believe I'm saying yes to this. Okay, we have a deal." He snapped the ticket book shut. "Hang tight while I run and get Samson."

"Prissy and I will wait right here."

"Uh-huh."

With her arm slung around the alpaca's neck, Remy grinned after Wyatt's retreating back. She resisted the urge to gloat. Until he was out of earshot. Then she said in a breezy tone, "Lovely doing business with you, Wyatt."

He continued on his way without showing the slightest sign of hearing her. But he'd barely made the turn onto Main Street when her phone dinged with an incoming text. You owe me a new shirt.

And that, Remy decided, was how to get in the last word.

Chapter Two

With nearly an hour chewed up by a sassy alpaca and her equally frustrating owner, Wyatt was up against the clock. He entered Samson's day care at a speed that would have set a terrible example if any kids were around. Thankfully, the reception area was empty. Except for the teenager manning the front desk.

Wyatt slowed to a respectful gait and greeted the girl. "Hi, Darlene."

"Hi, Sheriff. Wow, you made good time." She gave him a smile. "Hope you didn't break any speed limits getting over here."

He laughed at the bad joke. "Not a single one." Although he'd thought about it. Traveling on foot had kept him honest. "I'm here to pick up my nephew."

"Yeah, I heard." She gave him an apologetic grimace, zeroed in on Prissy's handiwork, then quickly looked away. "Mrs. Corbett has Samson in her office."

"Thanks. I know the way." Which was a testament to how often Wyatt made the trek from reception desk to the administrator's domain in the back of the building.

Despite his urgency, Wyatt found himself pausing on

the threshold of Mrs. Corbett's office. The sight of his nephew slumped in a chair grabbed Wyatt by the throat.

For a moment, he just stood there, rooted to the spot by a deep, undefined ache in his chest. He could read dejection in Samson's body. The evidence showed in the kid's lowered head, hunched shoulders and the fast tapping of his little sneakered feet.

Wyatt had done so many things wrong in the past year. Samson would not be one of them.

Letting out a fast breath, Wyatt stepped into the office. He nodded to the woman sitting behind the desk, then focused solely on his nephew. "Hey, little man."

Samson's head whipped up. "Uncle Wyatt!" Relief lit in the moss-green eyes. "You came."

Wyatt winced at the implication underneath the boy's words. Was Samson still so unsure of him? "You bet I came."

The boy launched himself out of the chair.

Hard to believe he could move so fast. But Wyatt was used to Samson's reckless abandon. He caught the boy against his chest and simply held on for several beats. It never ceased to amaze Wyatt how much he loved his nephew, with a fierceness that still caught him off guard.

The sound of a chair scraping across the tiled floor reminded him why he was here.

Eyes stinging slightly, he set the boy away from him, then held up his hand to stop the day care administrator from coming any closer. "Give us a second."

She halted with a frown.

Wyatt smiled down at his nephew, silently looking for any cuts or bruises that would explain away his behavior or cause additional concern. He saw none. It was his turn to blink in relief.

"Uncle Wyatt, what happened to your shirt?"

"It's nothing. Just a little alpaca spit."

"Did you arrest the alpaca?"

Wyatt's lips twitched at the image of Prissy spending a few hours in the county jail. "Out of my jurisdiction."

"Oh." With his face scrunched in confusion, the boy was—pun intended—the spitting image of his late father. He'd inherited his mother's light brown hair and vivid imagination, as well as her total lack of discipline. The latter both baffled and concerned Wyatt. CiCi hadn't been a bad person, just a terrible judge of character. She'd consistently chosen friends that led her into trouble. She was in prison now, and—

Mrs. Corbett cleared her throat.

Wyatt gave the woman his full attention.

She opened her mouth to speak, but Samson beat her to the punch. "Can we go now, Uncle Wyatt? I really, really want to go. Like. Right. Now."

The boy was looking at him with the hope of the wrongfully accused and Wyatt was Superman, Spider-Man and Batman all rolled into one. At the moment, he felt more like the Joker. "We'll leave once I'm finished speaking with Mrs. Corbett."

Taking her cue, the woman moved out from behind her desk. She glanced at Samson briefly, sighed, then shook her head. "I don't know what got into the boy. He's never made threats like that before."

"Threats?" He looked at his nephew. "What kind of threats?"

Samson took grave interest in his shoes. "It was nothing."

"I'm going to need you to be more specific."

When the boy continued studying his feet, Mrs. Corbett reentered the conversation. "Well," she began carefully.

"Samson said…" She faltered. Then passed the baton to the boy. "I think it's best if he tells you himself."

Wyatt rested a hand on his nephew's shoulder, light and nonthreatening. "All right, out with it. What did you say, Samson?"

"I…" The boy sighed, his expression bleak, as though he balanced the weight of the world on his seven-year-old shoulders. "I *may* have said I was going to blow up the day care."

Wyatt blinked. Samson had threatened to *blow up* the day care? That didn't make any sense. The boy was creative and showed unprecedented resourcefulness when he set his mind on a task. But he was not, nor had he ever been, violent. "Why would you say something like that?"

"I didn't really mean it. You gotta believe me, Uncle Wyatt. I would never blow up the day care." He flicked a glance at Mrs. Corbett. "Not with kids inside."

"Let's back up a second," Wyatt said as he attempted to sort through the garbled confession. "If you didn't mean you wanted to blow up the day care, what *did* you mean?"

The boy squared his shoulders. "This place needs an update and I have ideas. We'll need to knock out walls and stuff, like they do on those house fixer-upper-remaker shows."

Aha. Wyatt understood the situation now. Samson's mother used to love watching those house fixer-upper-remaker shows. She almost always had one on the screen while Samson played on the floor at her feet.

Clearly, the boy had been paying attention to the finer points of remodeling. "Let me get this straight," he said to Samson. "You want to renovate the day care, not blow it up."

"Well, yeah. I have the plans drawn up and everything. Want to see them?"

Actually, Wyatt did want to take a look. "Not right now." He switched his attention to Mrs. Corbett. "What we have here is a misunderstanding."

"Agreed. Which is why Samson is only suspended for the rest of the day. He can come back tomorrow, if he promises to stop all this nonsense about tearing down walls, and never, *ever* mentions—" she commanded the boy's stare "—blowing up the day care again."

"No, ma'am. I surely won't."

Wyatt let out a long, slow breath. "For my part, I'll make sure Samson understands the consequences of his words."

The woman bristled. "I'm sure I don't have to tell you what will happen if he doesn't."

"No, ma'am. You don't." Wyatt touched his nephew's shoulder. "Grab your backpack. We're leaving now."

"Okay." The boy happily followed Wyatt out of the building. He waited until they were safely on the move before asking, "Am I in big trouble, Uncle Wyatt?"

Wyatt bit back a sigh at the boy's miserable tone. "We'll talk about it later."

"Are you taking me to jail?"

This time, Wyatt did sigh. The question hit a little too close to home. "I'm not arresting you, Samson. But we will be having a long discussion about the difference between blowing up a building and renovating it."

"Now?"

"Not now." Wyatt glanced at his watch. If Remy was indeed waiting outside her clinic, he could still make his meeting with the mayor on time.

He picked up the pace.

Samson trotted along beside him. "Why are we in a hurry?"

"I have an important meeting to go to. But first, I'm taking you to spend the afternoon with Miss Remy."

"Miss Remy?" The boy looked confused, but only for a moment. "Oh…you mean, the pretty animal doctor?"

"That's the one."

"I like her." Samson picked up the pace, but then came to an abrupt stop. "Wait. Will Miss Remy's nieces be there?"

Something in the kid's expression had Wyatt recalling a brief encounter between his nephew and one of Remy's twin nieces at the Latte Da. Words had been exchanged. Apologies grudgingly given, but only after considerable prompting. "Miss Remy's nieces won't be there. Just you."

"Okay, good." Samson resumed walking—his steps considerably lighter. And faster. Which suited Wyatt just fine.

They took the corner leading to the back of Remy's building at top speed, whereby Wyatt discovered the woman waiting exactly where he'd left her. Prissy, looking deceptively innocent, stood next to her.

Samson got a good look at the alpaca, let out a happy whoop and took off at a dead run.

Remy had nearly given up on Wyatt returning anytime soon when he came around her building, his nephew scuttling along by his side. The sheriff looked annoyed and harried. The thrilled little boy practically flew in her direction, shouting out her name and waving his arms enthusiastically above his head.

At least one of them was excited to see her. Not bad odds. Not terribly great ones, either. Story of her life.

Remy came from a large family of overachievers. She had four brothers, two of them medical doctors. Another one was a former Air Force pilot turned successful multibusiness owner, and then there was the world-class, internationally acclaimed artist. But it was her perfect older sister whom Remy was compared with most often. And almost always found wanting, more now that she'd moved from Denver back to Thunder Ridge after her fiancé dumped her.

Why was it, she wondered, that she always seemed to come in second best? A question she set aside the moment Samson stopped just short of plowing into her. He grinned up at her, displaying a missing front tooth. "Hey, Miss Remy."

"Hey, yourself."

The grin widened. Remy smiled back, mildly smitten. Samson was a cute little boy. He had a face full of freckles beneath an unruly mop of light brown hair. He currently wore a superhero T-shirt streaked with a smear of brown that she hoped was dried mud. As the proud owner of a ten-acre ranch she'd acquired upon returning to Thunder Ridge, Remy couldn't help but consider other possibilities.

Samson's jeans were also stained with unidentifiable brown smudges. But at least his backpack was clean, as were his sneakers, both of which were untied.

"Who's that?" Samson asked, pointing to the alpaca.

"This—" Remy patted the animal "—is my friend Prissy. She lives with me on my ranch."

Samson's eyes widened with unabashed interest. "Is she nice? Can I pet her?"

"Yes, to both questions." Remy took the boy's hand and guided it to Prissy's neck. "You want to go in the same direction each time you stroke her, not back and forth. See? Like this."

Still holding Samson's hand, she demonstrated the proper motion. By the time the boy had the technique mastered, Wyatt had joined them. Remy hadn't actually heard him come up behind her, but she could smell him.

Fresh sunshine with a side of spicy male. Her heart did a little kick. She really liked how Wyatt smelled.

She breathed in deeply.

The world seemed to pause, and Remy couldn't catch her breath. Then, her pulse skittered back to life, giving her another, harder jolt. She glanced over her shoulder and caught Wyatt standing entirely too close. The bright afternoon light had turned his sun-kissed hair a burnished copper and his eyes a light, golden shade of amber.

Some unnamed emotion spread through her. Something that had to do with the man himself. Wyatt was the physical embodiment of raw masculine power. Authority radiated off him like a second skin, and he always kept his word. A woman could rely on a man like him. He would never lead her along for two years. Then toss her over for his campaign manager because the other woman fit his ideal of a politician's wife better than Remy.

No, Wyatt Holcomb was nothing like her ex-fiancé.

As if drawn by the same invisible cord, Wyatt leaned closer. She leaned toward him.

"Am I doing this right?"

Samson's question had them jerking apart. Remy swung back around to study the boy's petting technique. "Perfect. You're a natural."

The boy beamed under her praise. "I love animals."

Remy ruffled his hair. "Kid after my own heart. One day, I'll introduce you to my ferret."

"You have a ferret?"

"Yep, and a potbellied pig. A whole bunch of stray barn cats that come and go, and a Great Dane named Scooby. I also have a Shetland pony."

Samson nearly bounced out of his shoes. "Are they all here now?"

"At my ranch."

"Oh."

Wyatt's cell phone chose that moment to ding. He studied the screen a moment, then said, "Gotta go." He swept his gaze over Remy's face. "We're good here?"

She resisted the urge to roll her eyes. Had he not been paying attention? "We're good."

He remained immobile.

"Buh-bye, Wyatt. Go on. Go." She made a shooing motion with her hands. "Meeting. Mayor. Can't be late. Any of this ringing a bell?"

"All of it." Still, he hesitated.

Remy blew out a frustrated breath. "We got this, don't we, Samson?"

The boy gave her a distracted thumbs-up.

At last, Wyatt turned to go. He looked back only once. Okay, twice. Remy waved both times.

She waited until he was completely out of sight before winking at the boy by her side. "Phew, I thought he'd never leave."

Samson laughed.

"Now." Remy steered the boy to a picnic table and waited for him to sit before doing so herself. "Tell me what happened at day care today. And don't leave out a single detail."

As if he'd been waiting for a chance to tell his side of the story, Samson unloaded the entire incident one step at a time.

When he finally wound down, Remy understood why he'd been sent home. She also understood Samson better. Perhaps he could have chosen a different way to present his ideas to his teacher. But, wow, the kid had a highly advanced way of looking at the world. "Please tell me you still have the plans for your reimagined day care."

Samson nodded enthusiastically. "They're in my back-pack."

"Well, let's see what you got."

Within seconds, the contents of his backpack were laid out on the table and Samson was rummaging through a collection of crumpled papers. Remy recognized the par-aphernalia of a seven-year-old's typical day. Art projects, school assignments, a spelling test with a lot of red marks on it. Finally, Samson located the plans for his dream day care.

He spread out the large piece of butcher's paper and turned it toward Remy. She studied the series of meticu-lously drawn rectangles, squares and a few pentagons. The boy had connected the shapes in a sort of symbiotic way that was both quirky and yet made an odd sort of sense.

"Amazing," she whispered. It was no exaggeration. What really impressed her was how much the picture re-sembled an architect's actual blueprints, measurements and all. Samson wasn't just smart. He was brilliant. A prodigy. Did Wyatt know this about his nephew?

"You have a real talent, kid." Remy couldn't keep the awe out of her voice.

Samson's dream day care looked like, well, a day care. As imagined by a brilliant seven-year-old boy. He'd paid close attention to the play areas. And had included built-in tables along the walls for snack time plus other activi-ties that required a flat surface. "What's this?" she asked.

"An indoor track so we can ride our bikes anytime, even in the winter."

"Smart." The cubbies came with compartments for all the essentials, including water bowls for pet turtles. There were no offices or break rooms for the teachers, which didn't surprise Remy. A little boy wouldn't think of those.

"You really like it?" he asked her, uncertainty buzzing from every pore.

"I *love* it."

Samson smiled, but just as quickly his face fell, and he ran his finger across the top edge of the paper. "My teacher hated it."

Remy saw red. What sort of educator told a kid she hated his work? "Your teacher actually said she hated this?"

"Not exactly." He continued dragging his finger across the paper. "She said I was wasting my time drawing rectangles and squares when I should be working on my spelling. She could be right." He produced a sheepish grin that stole Remy's heart. "I'm a pretty bad speller."

As evidenced by the red marks on the test Remy pretended she hadn't seen. She'd been a bad speller at Samson's age. No shame in that. Plenty of time to fix it. She suddenly wanted to pull the boy into her arms. She didn't. It would hurt too much and remind her of all she didn't have. She patted his hand instead. "How about we head inside and rustle us up a snack?"

"Do you have gummy bears?"

"Do I have gummy bears?" Remy scoffed at the question. "You, my two-legged little friend, are looking at the number-one gummy bear authority in all of Thunder Ridge."

"Oh, yeah?" The gleam in Samson's eyes was 100 percent boy. "Prove it."

Chapter Three

Wyatt's meeting with the mayor went long. He still wasn't sure what to think about his new boss. Sutton Wentworth had been clear on her commitment to keep spending at an all-time low. No budgetary decisions were getting rubber-stamped by her—or anyone else in her office. After that little pointed lecture, Wyatt hadn't been surprised she'd held off approving his request for a new deputy. But she hadn't turned him down, either. He could expect her final decision after she reviewed the data more closely, she'd said.

From that interaction alone, Wyatt predicted a long, bumpy road with Mayor Wentworth. Again, not all that surprising. Sutton had graduated from Thunder Ridge High three years ahead of him. Back then she'd been Sutton Fowler, senior class president, editor of the yearbook and captain of the cheerleaders. As the youngest elected mayor in Thunder Ridge's history, Sutton was still aiming for the fences.

Good for her. Potentially bad for Wyatt. Especially if she followed through on her campaign promises via his budget. Checking his watch, he picked up the pace. If he stayed focused, he could knock off a few more tasks before the end of the workday.

Because his afternoon hadn't been filled with enough conflict, Doris met him at his office door. She swept one long, assessing glance over him and sighed heavily. "You blew it with the mayor."

"Too soon to tell," he admitted. "We're in a holding pattern until further notice."

"A holding pattern? That's what you kids call stone-walling these days?"

Wyatt did not respond to the dry tone, or the thinly veiled insult. When Doris was on one of her tirades, it was best to let her go. Then again, Wyatt was not the ten-year-old boy she'd caught with contraband fireworks on the Fourth of July anymore. He was the town sheriff. About time he started acting like it. "I have everything under control."

"We need that extra deputy, Sheriff."

No one knew this better than Wyatt. But Doris was not a woman to be ignored, so he said in a calm, appeasing tone, "I'm aware. And would you look at the time? It's after four. I have a few things to finish before I can pick up Samson."

One painfully long moment later, Doris managed a short nod and a pleasant, "Have a lovely evening with your nephew."

An hour and twenty minutes later, Wyatt entered the animal clinic Remy shared with the other veterinarian in town. The waiting area was empty. After stuffing his sunglasses in his front pocket, he moved closer to the reception desk. Which was *not* empty.

Remy's partner, Dr. Grace Elliott, sat in the lone chair, her gaze riveted to the computer screen. The receptionist—Wyatt forgot his name—stood behind her, hands on his hips, a distressed look on his face. "I don't know what happened, Doc. It just froze up on me."

"I think I see what's wrong." Grace worked the keyboard with the speed and efficiency of someone who knew her way around computers.

Wyatt cleared his throat.

"Be right with you." Grace's fingers continued flying across the keys.

The veterinarian was a few years older than Remy. She had a wiry, athletic build and kept her blond hair spiky short. She wore a pair of thick, black-rimmed eyeglasses that made her look like a computer nerd. Word around town was that Grace was good with animals, not so much with people. Her fledging practice had taken off only after Remy had moved back to town six months ago.

Wyatt cleared his throat again. "I'm looking for Dr. Evans and my nephew."

"They're in the break room. Go through that door." The receptionist made a vague gesture to his left. "Then hitch a hard right once you come to the hallway."

"Thanks." Completely alone with his thoughts for the first time all day, Wyatt searched for a reason that would explain Samson's recent behavior. The acting out had started only a few weeks ago. Had there been a specific event that caused the change in the boy? Or was it a series of small resentments that had finally boiled over?

Wyatt simply didn't know. Following the sound of voices, he entered what looked like a break room. The microwave and bag of half-eaten gummy bears were a dead giveaway, as was the round table and chairs where Remy and Samson sat working on a project. They hadn't noticed Wyatt yet.

With Remy looking on, Samson scribbled across a large piece of paper. The boy's hair stuck out in tufts, the way it always did when he forgot to comb it before leaving for school.

"What about putting it there?" she asked, pointing to the right-hand corner of the page.

"Good idea." Tongue caught between his teeth, Samson bent over and went to work, his pencil flying across the page.

When his hand stopped moving, Remy said, "Nice addition. Give it up, dude."

Grinning, Samson bumped his fist against hers. "What next?"

An animated discussion ensued.

Wyatt's heart filled with affection. Remy was good with Samson. Really good. She also looked really good. Earlier in the day, she'd been the picture of tidy professionalism. Her white lab coat hadn't shown a single wrinkle and her hair had been perfectly smooth across her head. Now, her lab coat was nowhere to be found and several long, silky black strands had escaped the sleek ponytail to curve across her cheek.

Something stronger than affection moved through Wyatt at the sight of Remy's disheveled state, something he didn't want to analyze too closely. His mind took a journey through the past instead. Remy had always been there, in his head, in his life, for as long as he could remember. From the tender age of five, he'd been best friends with her brother Brent. That had put Wyatt in close proximity with Remy, first as children, then as teens, then as young adults.

Even when they'd both left for college and she'd eventually settled in Denver, Wyatt had been aware of her presence when she came home for visits. That was the problem. He'd always been aware of her. Too aware.

He forced his mind back to the present.

"Sorry I'm late," he said. "Couldn't be helped."

"Did you have an emergency?" Remy asked, turning a concerned look his way.

"Nothing like that." He pushed away from the door-jamb. "My meeting with the mayor went long and then I had a few things that needed tying up."

"Ah." Now that she was looking at him, Wyatt couldn't break the connection. Not that he tried very hard. Remy's blue eyes, clear and penetrating, seemed to stare right into his soul, gently prying for answers to questions she hadn't voiced. But he needed asked.

It was a fanciful thought and one he shoved aside for that very reason.

"Come see what your nephew has been up to." She smiled as she spoke. Remy had a great smile. The kind that made a man take notice.

He tore his gaze away from all that messy hair and gleaming white teeth and general prettiness. Half sitting, half leaning against the table, Wyatt gave his nephew his undivided attention. "Whattya working on, little man?"

Samson beamed at the question. "It's a new set of plans for the day care."

"What happened to the old ones?"

The boy's distracted gaze angled up to Wyatt. "I had a different idea for the snack area. Miss Remy gave me more paper so I could start over."

"I keep extra around in case my nieces stop by," she explained, then added, "Your nephew has a lot of artis-tic talent."

Wyatt knew that. But he didn't respond. He couldn't. He was too busy swallowing past the lump in his throat. Samson's mother possessed more than her share of artistic talent. Every bit had gone unrealized. CiCi had been too undisciplined, wildly unfocused and easily manipulated by others. Wyatt was terrified Samson would follow in his mother's footsteps.

He knew—logically—that not all artists lost their way

and became drug addicts. Remy's older brother McCoy was a prime example of how to be a success. Not only did people come from all over the world to see his Ice Castles at Christmastime, his photographs had won numerous international awards, including several IPAs.

"What do you think of my day care, Uncle Wyatt?"

He picked up the drawing and gave it a long, considering look. Remy was right. The boy had talent, even more than his mother had at Samson's age. It would be up to Wyatt to provide enough structure in the boy's life to prevent him from taking the wrong path. "I like it. Definitely a keeper."

"I think so, too." Satisfied with the praise, Samson began rolling up the paper as if it were a real set of blueprints. Wyatt was impressed. The boy really had been paying close attention to those fixer-upper shows.

"Can I say goodbye to Prissy before we go home?" Samson asked Remy, who responded without missing a beat, "She'd be insulted if you didn't."

Samson grinned.

Wyatt shook his head, muttering, "We wouldn't want to hurt the alpaca's feelings, now, would we."

Remy gave Wyatt the stink eye. "You did *not* just insult my sweet alpaca."

"Of course not."

"Correct answer." Remy dropped her gaze, which put her line of sight directly with the stain her sweet alpaca had given him. "Oh, Wyatt. Please tell me you didn't attend your meeting with the mayor wearing that shirt?"

"I believe the evidence speaks for itself."

A parade of emotions crossed her face. Chagrin, guilt, amusement. "No clean shirt available, huh?"

"No time to change." He frowned. "Where is the woolly menace on four legs, anyway?"

"Out back where *you* tied her up."

She said this as though Wyatt had manhandled the animal, which he most certainly had not. He'd been very gentle with Remy's *sweet alpaca*. "You're absolutely sure she's still hooked to the bike rack?"

"I…" Remy's gaze darted around the room, landing everywhere but on Wyatt. "Um. Yeah, pretty sure."

Her obvious lack of certainty had him rubbing at the headache pounding behind his eyes. "You better be right."

"I usually am."

Such a Remy response. "Not much for modesty, are you, Dr. Evans?"

"Oh, I hit the mark every once in a while." She batted her eyelashes. "When I concentrate real hard."

Another typical Remy response.

"Can I go say goodbye to Prissy now?" Samson asked.

Grateful for the interruption, Wyatt took charge of the situation. "Grab your gear," he told the boy. "We'll leave out the back way."

Remy hopped to her feet and scrambled to the doorway. "Let me walk you out."

"No need to trouble yourself," Wyatt said. "I know the way."

"It's no trouble, really." Something crossed her face. Indecision? Guilt? A complete lack of confidence in her obstinate animal? "I need to check on a few things out back, anyway."

They both knew what *things* needed checking on. Clearly, Remy wanted to make sure Prissy was behaving herself.

The odds were not in the alpaca's favor.

Hoofing it double time to the back door, Remy exited the animal clinic five steps ahead of Wyatt. She let out a quick sigh of relief when she saw Prissy noshing on a patch of grass. Although Remy would never admit this out loud, especially not within the hearing of a certain sheriff, no good would come from Prissy wandering through town.

The alpaca could get lost, or hit by a car, or mauled by a coyote, or any number of tragic endings. An involuntary shudder moved along Remy's spine at the thought of the horrific possibilities that could befall her alpaca.

Tucking her concerns behind a carefree smile, Remy addressed the animal in a calm, soothing voice. "Prissy, come say goodbye to Samson."

The alpaca lifted her head at a painfully slow pace that would put any self-respecting snail to shame. Still chewing, she eyed Remy with an impassive look, as if to say, "What? Now? Can't you see I'm busy?"

That was just the kind of prissy attitude that had earned the alpaca her name. Catching sight of Wyatt, the animal abandoned her afternoon snack and sauntered over in his direction, intent in her gaze.

With one large, rather giant, purposeful step, he moved out of spitting distance.

Smart man.

Accepting rejection with grace and dignity, the alpaca switched directions and ambled over to Samson. She nuzzled the boy's cheek.

"Awww." Samson wrapped his arms around Prissy's neck and buried his face in the fur. "I love you, too."

Seizing the moment, Wyatt tugged Remy a few steps away from the mutual lovefest. "I want to thank you for watching Samson this afternoon. You saved the day."

"He's a great kid, Wyatt. It was my pleasure, really. If you ever need me to watch him again, you just have to ask, okay?"

He nodded, then glanced over to where Samson carried

on a heartfelt, one-sided conversation with Prissy. Wyatt's eyes narrowed ever so slightly. Never a good sign. "Fix the animal's pen, Remy. I mean it." He slid his gaze back to her face. "No more free passes. Next time—"

"Yeah, yeah, I know." She pitched her voice to a low, stern octave that mimicked his deep baritone. "Next time you catch Prissy wandering *your streets* you'll slap me with a five-hundred-dollar fine."

"Look at you, catching on at last. And it only took three attempts at reason and one threat of a hefty fine to get us on the same page."

"Funny guy. Ever consider taking your act on the road?"

His eyes crinkled and the laugh lines on either side of his mouth deepened, stealing her breath. "Not really, I'm happy with my current situation."

She couldn't help it. She laughed.

He joined in. It was genuine amusement, too. The sound was a little rusty, as if he didn't let himself laugh too often. But when he did? Wyatt was nothing short of devastating when he loosened up a little.

Softening toward him, Remy made a valiant attempt at taking the high road. "I'll fix Prissy's pen Sunday after church. You have my promise."

And just like that, the man's laughter vanished. His smile soon followed. "Why not sooner?"

She tried not to roll her eyes. Did the man know nothing about her life? "Because I'm booked solid with patients through the rest of the week and into Saturday morning. And before you ask about Saturday afternoon, I have to teach Puppy School."

"Puppy School?" Samson spun around to face them. Eyes wide, he asked, "What's Puppy School?"

"It's where I educate children like you how to care for

their new puppies. I hold it out on my ranch and—" She broke off at Wyatt's swift shake of his head.

"That sounds super fun," Samson said. "Can I come? I really like puppies. Like a lot. A lot, a lot."

Still shaking his head, Wyatt answered before Remy could. "You don't have a new puppy, Samson. So, you don't need Puppy School."

Samson was not to be deterred. "Couldn't we adopt one from the pound?"

"No puppy," Wyatt reiterated. "No Puppy School. I mean it." He swung a desperate plea in Remy's direction. "Help me out here."

She patted the poor man's arm in sympathy. "One of my brother's English bulldogs had a litter of puppies recently. I bet Casey would let Samson borrow one of them for class."

Wyatt made a face. "That's not what I meant." Then he went silent. A speculative gleam came in his eyes. That was one big bad brain working very quickly. "Tell you what. Samson can join your class and learn how to train a puppy that is not his, nor will ever be his, under any circumstances, ever." He said that last part while looking directly at the boy, who was currently vibrating with excitement. "And while he's doing that, I'll fix Prissy's pen myself."

Remy gaped at Wyatt. "You'd do that for me?"

"Not for you," he corrected. "For Thunder Ridge, in the name of law and order." Wyatt pulled his sunglasses out of his left shirt pocket. "What time should we arrive at your ranch on Saturday?"

"Um…" Remy realized she was still gaping at the man. Whenever she thought she had him figured out, he went and surprised her with stuff like offers to fix her animal pens. "Puppy School starts at two o'clock sharp."

"Good enough. Come on, Samson." Wyatt shoved the sunglasses in place. "Let's go home."

"Okay." Before falling into step beside his uncle, Samson ran over to Remy and gave her a hard hug. "Thanks for hanging out with me this afternoon. I had fun."

"I had fun, too."

"And thanks for inviting me to Puppy School."

"No problem." Remy stroked a lock of light brown hair from the boy's forehead. He had such a sweet face and seemed a little sad. That just tore at her heart. She wanted to hug him tighter, but she would only be torturing herself. She set him away from her. "See you Saturday."

Wyatt gave her one solid nod, completely ignored Prissy and then guided Samson down the alleyway toward Main Street. Remy smiled after the boy in his scuffed jeans half skipping, half running beside the man in his sheriff's gear. She tried not to notice how fit Wyatt looked in his uniform. She'd always had a thing for men in uniform. That man, anyway. She'd thought she'd grown immune over the years. She'd thought wrong.

Wyatt would make a great father to his own children one day. Something that felt like loss moved through Remy at the thought. Parenthood was a blessing she would probably never experience for herself. It wasn't impossible, or so her doctor claimed. Just improbable as Remy grew older. Her ex-fiancé had told her it didn't matter one way or the other. That they would adopt if it came to that. Remy had believed him.

Until he'd broken off their engagement two weeks after she'd shared the diagnosis. Doubt had eaten away at her self-confidence. Her sense of inadequacy had only dug deeper when Matt married his campaign manager weeks after demanding his ring back from Remy.

Six months later, she was still reeling from the shock of his betrayal.

As if sensing her sudden shift in mood, Prissy nuzzled Remy's cheek. She hugged the alpaca's neck and, like Samson, buried her face in the soft fur.

This, Remy decided, was why she preferred animals to people.

Animals loved unconditionally. They didn't put impossible expectations on a woman. Animals were loyal and incapable of betrayal. They didn't care about medical diagnoses. Or judge a woman unfit to be a future politician's wife because she might have difficulty conceiving.

"Come on, Prissy." Remy wiped at her eyes and repeated Wyatt's statement to Samson. "Let's go home."

Chapter Four

Wyatt found comfort in routine. He loved a good spreadsheet and considered a detailed to-do list a thing of beauty. In contrast, his sister hated schedules and timelines. *Consistency* was a dirty word to CiCi. As a result, Samson spent the first five and a half years of his life with very little discipline and even less stability.

To compensate, Wyatt now kept the boy on a tight schedule, especially in the evenings. No changes, no substitutions. Homework first, if any was assigned. Followed by a half hour of screen time, or bike riding, weather permitting. Then dinner. Next came a bath or shower—Samson's choice—teeth-brushing and, finally, bedtime and prayers. If the boy was under the covers by eight, Wyatt allowed another half hour of reading.

Once Samson was asleep, Wyatt caught up on work—he was always behind with paperwork.

Tonight, he wasn't in bed until well after midnight. It had been that kind of day. He managed one glorious hour of sleep before he woke with a start. Heart beating wildly against his ribs, he lay perfectly still, trying to pinpoint what had brought him fully awake. His mind went straight to Samson. Had the boy cried out? It wouldn't be the first time.

Feet bare, Wyatt padded down the hallway and peered into Samson's room. The boy was fast asleep, hugging his teddy bear for dear life. The covers were tangled at his feet.

Wyatt stood very still, ignoring the pain in his chest, the one that said he was failing the boy. What else explained Samson's recent acting out? If only Wyatt knew what he was doing wrong. What was he missing? Hands flexing at his sides, he approached the bed and gazed down at the child. He would slay dragons for Samson, real or imagined. Right now, though, the little boy looked at peace, not a care in the world, safe and secure in his bed. Relief nearly brought Wyatt to his knees.

Throat burning, he drew the covers back up to the boy's chin and whispered, "Love you, little man."

Samson mumbled something unintelligible in his sleep but didn't wake up.

On surprisingly unsteady legs, Wyatt left the room. Needing a moment to settle his racing heart, he descended the stairs and entered the kitchen. He wasn't hungry, so he continued through the mudroom and out the back door and settled on the back stoop to stare up at the dark, moonless sky.

Elbows resting on his knees, he blinked into the inky stillness and listened to the music of the night. The dark woods beyond his property line were never fully silent. Wind rustled through the trees. Nocturnal creatures cried out to one another. Lulled by the sound, Wyatt's mind wanted to wander. He let it cross over time, back to the phone call that had changed the trajectory of his life forever.

Even alone, with no one to see his tears, Wyatt kept that memory simple in his mind, no emotion, no visceral reaction to the news that his parents were dead. *A tragic boating accident, nothing to be done. They were gone in an instant. I'm sorry for your loss.*

He couldn't remember the rest of the call. He'd been in his second year playing pro football, still a rookie but proving himself on the field. CiCi had been barely fifteen at the time, about to enter her sophomore year of high school. There'd been no question what Wyatt would do. He came home. And his degree in criminology made him a perfect candidate for the sheriff's office.

The next three years had been rough on both him and CiCi. What did a twenty-three-year-old football player know about raising a teenage girl? Or, for that matter, being an officer of the law? As he'd attempted to split his time between work and parenting, he'd made mistakes. He'd done things right, too, but maybe not enough.

The door between the kitchen and the mudroom creaked on its hinges. "Uncle Wyatt?"

"Out here," he called, realizing he'd been sitting in the past for well over an hour. "On the back stoop."

Samson appeared in the doorway, hair sleep-mussed, one hand on the screen door, the other holding his teddy bear. He looked so small and alone. It was the fear in the boy's eyes that had Wyatt's heart racing.

"You couldn't sleep, either?" he asked.

Samson shook his head. "I had a bad dream."

The misery in the words had Wyatt battling back a fresh round of sorrow. "Come on." He patted the empty space on the step beside him. "Sit down next to me."

Dragging the teddy bear up to his chest, Samson accepted the invitation with a soft plunk. As Wyatt reached up to smooth the tousled hair, he studied the boy more closely, noting the way he gnawed on his thumbnail, the way his eyes, shadowed with leftover fear, kept slipping to the ground, then back to Wyatt, then down again. "What did you dream about?" he asked softly.

"I don't remember."

Wyatt knew that wasn't true. They'd been through this before, too many nights to count. "Did you dream about your mother, again?"

The boy continued staring at his feet. "Maybe."

Translation, yes. And possibly the reason for Samson's change in behavior. The boy had been dreaming about his mother nearly every night for two weeks. With the dreams came memories, some good, some not so good. CiCi hadn't been a bad mother. Actually, she'd been a pretty good one. Until the night she'd crashed her car into a tree, killing Samson's father and putting herself in the hospital. A subsequent addiction to painkillers led to a series of bad decisions when it came to her son.

"I went to your room," Samson said, his fingers fiddling with the bear's nose. "You weren't there. I got scared."

The accusation in the boy's voice tore at Wyatt's composure. Pulling in a ragged breath, he slung an arm around Samson's shoulders and tugged him closer. "I would never leave you alone in the house. You know that, right?"

"I guess so."

Translation, no. Wyatt figured the boy was remembering another night, in another house.

"Samson." Wyatt spoke in a calm, but firm voice. "Look at me."

"I am looking at you."

He wasn't.

Wyatt kissed the top of the boy's head and said, very quietly, very seriously, "I will never leave you alone in the house, not ever. You have my word."

The little boy looked at him then, tears brimming in his eyes. "I would be really mad at you if you did."

"You'd be right to be mad at me."

Something sad and tortured moved in the boy's eyes. "Even if you didn't mean to scare me?"

"Even then." Wyatt knew they weren't talking about him, or the dream, but the night CiCi had left her son alone in their one-bedroom apartment so she could get high with a neighbor. Samson had been only five at the time, but he'd known to call Wyatt when he couldn't find his mom in their apartment.

Wyatt still remembered the fear he'd felt as he'd sped across town, not knowing what he'd find. He still felt the rage that had filled him when he'd located CiCi two doors down, strung out on the neighbor's couch, completely unaware of the danger she'd put her son in.

That had been the end of listening to CiCi's lies.

Wyatt had moved his sister and nephew into his house the next morning, then immediately checked CiCi into an outpatient treatment program. She'd gotten clean, or so Wyatt believed. Again, he'd been kidding himself. He'd found over one hundred grams of heroin in her possession. There'd been little choice but to arrest her for a Colorado level one felony. She was currently serving a mandatory three-year sentence in Denver's Women's Correctional Facility.

"Can I be mad at my mom?"

With a sigh, Wyatt nodded. "Yeah, little man, you can be mad at her."

"Okay, good."

"But, Samson, when your mom comes home," Wyatt added, needing to defend CiCi to her son, "she'll be well again, and you won't have to be mad at her anymore."

Samson seemed to consider this. Then slowly, almost reluctantly, he nodded. "I still love her and really, really miss her."

"Me, too."

They sat in silence after that. It wasn't often Wyatt didn't know what to do. But he really didn't know what to do. Not just in the next few minutes, but for the next two and half years while CiCi served out the rest of her prison sentence. A few sessions with a therapist probably wouldn't hurt Samson. Or Wyatt. He'd make that happen sooner rather than later.

"Uncle Wyatt?"

"Hmm?"

"Can I have some gummy bears before I go back to bed?"

And just like that, he had his nephew back. Eyes stinging, Wyatt forgot all about routines and schedules and appropriately healthy snacks. "You bet."

Friday afternoon, Remy left City Hall with a heavy dose of frustration nipping at her heels. Oh, sure. She'd heard the old adage *You can't fight City Hall*. Heard it, and scoffed, thinking whoever had coined the phrase hadn't met Remy Evans. They had, apparently, met Fiona Elliott.

It wasn't over, Remy told herself. Just a little speed bump on the road to success. Whatever it took, she would open her petting zoo on time. Failure was not an option. She needed the revenue to fund the down payment on her loan for the adjoining property to her ranch. She'd also scheduled field trips with church groups, summer camps and day care centers, two for the end of next week.

What she needed to do was find a workaround to Fiona's refusal to move Remy's application to the front of the line. She also needed a peppermint mocha—heavy on the mocha. She always thought better with a coffee in her hand.

She knew just the place. Her brother's coffee shop was the best in town, if he did say so himself. Which he did, often and to anyone within earshot. Humble, Casey Evans was not. She kind of loved that about her brother.

One block later, Remy stepped into the scent of roasting coffee and fresh-baked yeasty deliciousness. Cargo Coffee was, as always, packed with an eclectic mix of people sitting at tables, standing at the coffee bar or leaning against walls painted with large world maps.

Casey, the oldest of Remy's brothers, was working behind the counter, as was his custom every Friday afternoon. A former Air Force captain turned private cargo pilot, he'd inherited the entrepreneurial gene from their father. Remy hoped she'd inherited that same gene. She loved living in Thunder Ridge again and wondered why she hadn't come home sooner.

She knew, of course. Although Matt was a hometown boy himself, he hadn't wanted to live in Nowhere, Colorado—his words—when Denver was only fifty miles away.

What a shortsighted view. Remy should have known then and there things wouldn't work out between them.

Casey motioned her over to the coffee bar. It was only when she stepped in his direction that she realized he was talking to a well-built man in a sheriff's uniform. Yep, *that* man. Soft ripples of awareness moved through her. Feeling foolish and off balance, she gave Casey a brief shake of her head, then joined the line of people waiting to place their order at the cash register.

Unfortunately, Wyatt's voice carried over the low din of a dozen conversations. Or maybe she was just that attuned to his rich baritone. "I'm afraid it was strike three for the boy."

Strike three? That didn't sound good. Not if "the boy" was Samson. Remy stepped out of line and moved closer to Wyatt, who still hadn't noticed her.

"What's worse," Wyatt continued, his velvety voice filled with exasperation, "the day care administrator also expelled Samson from the summer program."

Remy gasped in outrage. "That poor boy."

Wyatt whipped his head around to glare at her. "Eavesdropping, Remy. Really?"

She slid in next to Wyatt at the counter. "What did Samson do that was bad enough to earn his third strike?"

Wyatt sighed. The sound was full of world-weary frustration. "Apparently, he brought a frog and two baby lizards inside the building, whereby he relocated them into a little girl's cubby."

"That doesn't sound too terrible."

"Wait for it. There's more," Casey said, looking slightly troubled, as if somehow Samson's actions hit a little too close to home. Odd. As far as Remy knew, Casey had never brought reptiles to school. Had he?

No, that had been her.

"Go ahead, Wyatt," Casey urged. "Tell my sister what little girl was on the receiving end of Samson's prank."

Wyatt's apologetic gaze met Remy's. "It was Kennedy."

"Kennedy?" Remy's stomach dropped to her toes. "As in my niece Kennedy?"

"*Our* niece," Casey corrected. "And, yes, *that* Kennedy."

Now she understood Casey's personal investment in the situation. All of Remy's siblings were protective of Kennedy and her identical twin sister, Harper. The girls hadn't been a part of the family for long, only since December when their aunt Hope had come to town looking for their absentee father after their mother had died of breast cancer.

There'd been a brief case of mistaken identity, but all had turned out well. Brent, their real father, had immediately quit his job with Doctors Without Borders and flown home. This time for good. Meanwhile, Hope and Remy's other brother, Walker, had fallen in love. Their wedding was next month.

Happy endings all around.

Unless you were a little girl terrified of frogs and liz-ards. "Is Kennedy okay?"

"She was a little shaken up at first," Wyatt admitted, in-cluding both Remy and Casey in his explanation. "But when she found out Samson was getting expelled, she begged the teachers not to send him home. Lots of tears were involved and, from what I was told, really started flowing when Sam-son was unceremoniously marched out of the play area."

"Sounds like Kennedy," Casey said, nodding in sym-pathy.

Remy agreed with her brother. That did sound like Ken-nedy. The little girl had a sweet, tender heart. She would definitely be more upset that Samson got in trouble than over an unexpected confrontation with frogs and lizards. "Where's Samson now?"

"With Doris."

"Oh, Wyatt. Please tell me you didn't leave him with your scary assistant?" Remy couldn't keep the dismay out of her voice. "What were you thinking?"

"Don't answer that," Casey said. "It's a trick question."

Remy scowled at the man who, like all her other sib-lings, shared her jet-black hair and pale blue eyes. "Thanks for the support."

He shrugged. "Just helping out a friend."

"Over your own sister?"

"That's another trick question," he said, pointing at Remy and making her feel like the runt of the litter. Noth-ing new there. Speaking of litters… "Can I count on you to supply three, maybe four extra puppies for my Puppy School tomorrow?"

"Don't I always come through for you?"

He did. Always. Casey's word was rock solid. Once given, he never took it back. Never. Three more people entered the coffee shop and one of his employees called out for his assistance. "Duty calls." With that, he went to help other customers.

Frowning after him, Remy shook her head, then turned back to Wyatt, still frowning. "You could have called me to help you out with Samson today."

"Didn't cross my mind."

Well, ouch. Pride stinging, she covered the hurt with a laugh. "Seriously, you could have called me."

"I figured you were busy seeing patients. And now, I have to get back to the office." He grabbed the to-go cup near his hand and headed for the exit.

Wyatt might be through with their conversation. Remy was not. She had a million questions, starting with the most obvious one. "What are you going to do about Samson?" she asked, trotting after the fast-moving lawman.

He didn't break stride, didn't look in her direction, just kept walking. Through the coffee shop, out the front door and then down the sidewalk. She kept pace every step of the way, but not without effort. "I'm going to have a long, serious talk with the boy about what constitutes appropriate items for show-and-tell. Nothing with a heartbeat."

Probably a good idea. "I meant, what are you going to do with Samson during summer break?"

"Find another program that will take him."

"Kind of short notice," she said, puffing out the words. Wyatt was a really fast walker. "Wasn't today the last day of school?"

"Yep."

The one-word answer came out deceptively calm. Remy had seen people at their wit's end. She'd seen people on the verge of breaking. She'd never seen Wyatt in either situation. Until now. "That's unfortunate."

He drew a hard breath and, if she wasn't mistaken, picked up speed. "It is very unfortunate."

Remy quietly studied him as they hurried along at twice the pace of normal human beings, wondering why her heart always took a hit whenever she was around this man. Sure, he was good-looking. Really good-looking. But that wasn't the reason. It was an inexplicable desire to comfort him, as if she could somehow provide a place of rest from the cares of the world.

Which made no sense. Wyatt was the town sheriff, competent in too many ways to count, a protector to the bone. He didn't need comforting. He needed child care.

And she needed a permit for her petting zoo. Suddenly, an idea came to her, a really brilliant idea.

Wyatt must have gotten a good look at her face, no doubt bright red from exertion, and mercifully slowed his steps. "What's going on in that mind of yours, Remy?"

"Can't a woman take a little afternoon stroll with a friend?"

"Not if that woman is you. You're thinking so hard I can hear the gears spinning." Wyatt drew to a stop. "Might as well tell me what's on your mind."

Dragging in air, she considered her next words carefully. "How much pull do you have at City Hall?"

"Depends. What department?"

"The one that issues licenses and permits and stuff like that." She was pretty sure it had a name, but she couldn't recall it at the moment.

"What kind of permit are we talking about? Spit it out, Remy."

"I'm opening a petting zoo. Grasshopper Grange will be—"

"Whoa, hold up." He cut her off. "People actually pay money to pet grasshoppers?"

"No." She resisted the urge to roll her eyes. "I just thought the name sounded fun."

"Okay, but that's not what's rolling around in your head and I'm pressed for time. Let's have it, Remy. Spit it out," he repeated.

The man really needed to work on his people skills. "Since you asked so nicely, I have a proposition for you."

"What kind of proposition?"

"If you put in a good word on my behalf at City Hall or, better yet, push my permit through ahead of the others, I'll help you out with Samson."

"Help me out, how?"

"He can hang with me until you register him for another summer program. I'll have him shadow me at the clinic, then assist me with the animals at the ranch after I finish seeing patients."

Wyatt was shaking his head before she finished speaking. "That doesn't sound very structured. Samson needs structure."

Said the man so rigid he made a two-by-four seem pliant. "He'll get structure. Lots of it. Animals require constant care on a regular basis at regular intervals."

Sighing, Wyatt rubbed a hand down his face. "How much is this going to cost me?"

Aware he wasn't saying no, Remy thought about her answer. It felt weird charging Wyatt for something she would do for free. Although, now that he'd mentioned payment, she could use the money for that down payment. "How much was the summer program going to cost you?"

He quoted what Remy considered an astronomical fee. "Tell you what. You do your thing at City Hall and I'll charge you half what you would have paid for that overpriced day care. What do you say? Do we have a deal?"

"You caught me at a desperate moment."

Sounded like perfect timing to her. "I'll take that as

a yes. We can discuss the details after Puppy School tomorrow."

"Yeah, okay. That'll work. Now I really do need to get back to the office."

"Wait, before you go. You'll want this." She dug out a business card from the depths of her tote bag and handed it to him.

"What is that?" he asked, eyeing the tiny rectangle with open suspicion.

"Fiona Elliott's business card. She's the clerk in charge of approving my permit. Go on." She waved the card under Wyatt's nose. "Take it."

He stuffed his hands in his pockets. "I know Fiona."

Of course he did. Wyatt had been working at the sheriff's department for the past twelve years. He probably knew everybody in town. "So, you'll talk to her?"

"I'll talk to her."

Pleasure coursed through her, but then she realized today was Friday. "When?"

"When I get to it," he said, sounding like a man pushed to his limit.

Remy being Remy, she pushed a little harder. "Today?"

"I'll see what I can do. Goodbye, Remy."

"Bye." Watching him go and thinking maybe she should get his agreement in writing, she pulled out her phone and tapped out a quick text. Will you talk to Fiona this afternoon?

No response.

A simple yes or no will do.

The dancing bubbles appeared at last. Then came his glorious, one-word answer. YES.

Triumph, at last. Smiling, Remy filled another text with

three big red hearts. Before she pressed Send, she scrolled through the list of emojis on her phone and stopped at the "animals and nature" section. Chuckling softly, she added three miniature alpacas to the text, included three more red hearts for good measure, then pressed Send.

The dancing bubbles appeared immediately. They disappeared and, this time, stayed gone. Good. Finally, Remy had left Wyatt speechless.

Chapter Five

Wyatt entered his office still frowning at his phone. Where had Remy found an emoji that looked like an alpaca? Or maybe it was a llama. The picture was too small to know for sure. Still, it was pretty clever. A grin toyed at the edges of his lips. The woman definitely kept him on his toes. She'd always been a step ahead of him, for as long as he could remember. It wasn't an altogether awful sensation.

"You might want to wipe that smile off your face, Sheriff." Doris moved directly in his path, reached out and, before he knew what she was about to do, wrestled the coffee out of his fist.

"Hey, I was drinking that."

"You have bigger problems than your current lack of caffeine." She dropped the cup in the waste bin by her desk. "The mayor is waiting for you in your office. She does not look happy."

Wyatt forgot all about his coffee. "Do you know what she wants?"

"No." Doris gave him a get-real lift of her eyebrows. "That's above my pay grade."

That hadn't stopped her from gathering intel before.

"I set Samson up in the conference room. He's working on a very important—" she made air quotes "—*drawing*. Enough stalling, Sheriff. The mayor is a busy woman. It wouldn't be wise to keep her waiting."

"Copy that." Wyatt entered his office with an apology forming in his mind. "Did we have an appointment? Am I late?"

"Not at all." Sutton spun away from the window and smiled. She wore a dark business suit over a crisp white blouse. Adding to the image of a powerful woman, she'd pulled her platinum blond hair back in a tight bun that showed off her high cheekbones. "I was in the neighborhood and thought I'd stop by."

Given that her office was in the building next door, the illustrious mayor of Thunder Ridge was pretty much always in the neighborhood. "What can I do for you?"

"Actually, it's what I can do for you." An interesting lead-in, and one Wyatt hoped meant good news for his department.

"Well, then. Have a seat." He motioned to the lone visitor chair in his office, then rounded the desk and took his own seat.

Sutton did as he requested, her back ramrod straight. No doubt about it, the woman was a force to be reckoned with. A war widow, single mother and former trial attorney in New York City, she'd won the mayoral election in a landslide. She was also smart, savvy and dedicated to Thunder Ridge.

On paper, she was the kind of woman Wyatt should find attractive. And maybe he would have in another life. But whenever he thought about women the way a *man* thought about a *woman*, it wasn't Sutton's image that ever came to mind. It was Remy's.

He shook away the thought. "As I stated at our previous meeting, Ms. Mayor—"

"Wyatt, please. Even if your nephew wasn't my son's best friend, you and I went to high school together. Call me Sutton. In fact—" she gave him the toothy smile that had won over a lot of naysayers during her campaign "—I insist."

"All right. Sutton." He returned her smile. "Can I assume this is about my budget?"

She nodded. "I've reviewed the numbers and looked at all the other data you provided. You're right, Wyatt. Thunder Ridge needs another deputy, preferably one with experience. I'm approving your request." She stood abruptly, straightened her jacket with a tidy snap. "You may begin recruiting immediately."

Wyatt scrambled to his feet and shoved out his hand. "Thank you, Sutton."

"No, Wyatt. Thank you. Your data and attention to detail made my decision easy. As we're both busy people, I won't keep you any longer." She turned to go.

"Let me walk you out." Wyatt rounded his desk and caught up with her at the door.

She paused. "Although it's not my place to tell you how to do your job, I'd like to make one request concerning your new hire."

"Of course." He held her gaze and waited.

"Find the best candidate for the position, without regards to gender, age or life situation."

Aside from that being the law, Wyatt definitely wanted to hire the best deputy possible. "Goes without saying."

"And yet, I said it anyway."

They shared a laugh.

Wyatt promised to keep her posted on the search, then they went their separate ways, Sutton to her office and

Wyatt to check on Samson before passing on the good news to Doris. The moment he entered the conference room, the little boy looked up from the table. "Hey, Uncle Wyatt. Want to see my newest day care?"

"I sure do." Wyatt studied the drawing. This particular plan was more elaborate than the others. Most notably Samson had added a large glass dome. "What's this for?"

"Stargazing," Samson told him.

"You plan to attend day care at night?"

Samson laughed. "I would if there was a glass dome for stargazing."

"Can't say I blame you." Wyatt pointed to another detail. "What are these?"

"Chairs for spinning. Like this." Samson demonstrated the technique in the wheeled office chair. "Am I still in trouble for what happened with Kennedy today?"

"We'll talk about that later." Wyatt would save the lecture for tonight when he didn't have a half-dozen pressing items on his mind. He would also wait until then to tell the boy about "hanging out" with Remy next week.

"Are we going home now?"

"Not yet." Wyatt handed the paper back to Samson. "I have a few things to finish up."

"Okay." The boy went back to his project.

Impressed with the kid's focus, Wyatt made one more detour before returning to his office. Ten minutes later, after giving Doris the good news about their new deputy, he was sitting behind his desk, reviewing what he'd just learned. The information he'd gleaned from Fiona Elliott may or may not please Remy.

The city clerk had been reasonable, but firm. Remy's permit would get Fiona's attention in the order that it had arrived. Not a second sooner. On the bright side, Remy had filled out the form properly. Her check had cleared. And there were only two applications ahead of hers.

Wyatt had made good on his end of the bargain. He would throw his weight around only if it came to that. Remy was, after all, helping him out with Samson. Wyatt owed her. He was a man who always paid his debts.

Now that his nephew was on his mind, he opened the search engine on his computer and spent the next thirty minutes scrolling through the various summer camps in Thunder Ridge. The first two he found were full. The next two even more expensive than the one Samson would no longer be attending. Wyatt continued scrolling. Nothing seemed right.

He needed a break.

Mourning the coffee Doris had confiscated earlier, he went in search of a fresh cup from the break room. While he drank, he took the opportunity to scroll through emails on his phone. Upon his return, he found his assistant barring the entrance to his office again. She did not look happy. Of course, Doris rarely looked happy.

"You have another visitor," she said, looking at him with raised eyebrows.

"Who is it?"

"You'll find out soon enough."

Instincts humming, Wyatt braced himself, stepped across the threshold and…

Stopped cold. Of course, he thought. *Of course.*

Remy stood at his desk, back facing him, seemingly absorbed with the task of writing on a small sticky note. For a second, he simply stared.

His heart took a quick, hard thump at the sight she made, looking all fresh and female. He tried to remember if she'd been wearing the same clothes earlier that afternoon. Didn't seem likely. He would have remembered Remy looking like summer personified in a pair of white jeans, a sky blue sleeveless top and high-heeled sandals that revealed bright pink toenails. The same color as Prissy's bridle.

The woman clearly had a thing for pink. "Remy?"

She spun around. "Oh, Wyatt. Hi. I was just leaving you a note. Guess I don't have to now." Smiling, she crumpled the piece of paper into a tight ball, then sailed it through the air for a two-pointer in the trash can.

"Nice shot," he said.

"I know, right?" Still smiling, she stepped away from his desk and moved within inches of where he stood rooted to the spot. She was close enough now for him to get a good whiff of her perfume. A pleasant mix of lavender and vanilla, and Remy herself. "Aren't you going to ask me why I'm here?"

"Okay..." He swallowed. "Why are you here?" He swallowed again. "And why were you leaving me a note when your usual mode of communication is texting?"

"You can't delete a note as easily as a text."

That was patently untrue, as evidenced by her impressive two-pointer. That meant only one thing. She'd come to see if he'd followed through on his promise to look into her permit. "I heard you were at City Hall about an hour ago. And before you ask how I know, Doris told me."

"What else did Doris tell you?"

"That you have a packed schedule the rest of the day and I have exactly five minutes to state my business."

Wyatt decided to give Doris a big fat raise, out of his own pocket.

"Well?" Remy asked. "Did you speak to Fiona while you were at City Hall?"

"I did."

"Okay, good." Her smile brightened. Wyatt's head grew light. He couldn't stop noticing how pretty she looked in that blue top the same color as her eyes. He tried to focus on their conversation, not on the fact that his heartbeat had picked up speed, or that he experienced a flash of insight, as if he were on the verge of something life-changing.

"Come on, Wyatt. Don't keep me in suspense. Am I opening Grasshopper Grange in time for the summer rush?"

Before he could answer, Doris stepped into the office and, staring straight at Remy, said, "Time's up, dear." She swung around to look at Wyatt. "Your four thirty is here."

As far as Wyatt knew, he didn't have a four thirty. That didn't mean Doris hadn't scheduled an appointment. As his assistant was fond of saying, "I fill your calendar. It's up to you to check it on a regular basis." Which Wyatt often failed to do.

"Thanks, Doris."

Nodding, the administrative assistant took her cue and left the room.

"Time for you to go, too, Remy." With a touch to her arm, Wyatt showed her to the door and then, with a gentle nudge, sent her across the threshold.

"What about my permit?"

"It's being processed."

"What does that mean?"

"It means," he said, "you'll get your approval sometime early next week."

His response clearly wasn't good enough. Remy launched into a request for more information. Mouth grim, Wyatt nudged her a step back. Then shut the door in the middle of her petition. Problem solved. With a fast turn on his heel, he went to prepare for his appointment.

Mouth gaping open, Remy stood outside Wyatt's office fuming.

For several seconds, she blinked at the slab of institutional-grade wood mere inches from her face. He actually shut the door in her face!

She would not—could not—let that stand.

Throwing back her shoulders, she reached for the door handle. Then froze at the sound of a female clicking her tongue. "I wouldn't do that if I were you."

Remy continued staring at the closed door. "Why not?"

"Sheriff Holcomb has a long fuse, but once you light it, you better run in the opposite direction."

She swung around fast. "Are you saying Wyatt's temper can turn ugly?"

"Shame on you, Remy Evans. Don't go putting words in my mouth." Doris wagged her finger. "Sheriff Holcomb is a good man. One of the best I know."

Not many things scared Remy. Alligators didn't scare her. She actually thought they were kind of cute. She wasn't afraid of snakes. People didn't especially frighten her. Actually, Remy could go toe-to-toe with just about anyone.

Anyone, that was, except Doris McCook.

The woman petrified her. But still. "You saw what that man did to me. He shut the door in my face."

Doris arched a pair of matching eyebrows tweezed to the very edge of their existence. "Technically, Remy, Sheriff Holcomb did not shut the door in your face."

"Maybe not *technically*." She'd forgotten how literal this woman could be. "But if I'd been standing two inches closer I'd be fishing splinters out of my nose right about now."

Doris's lips might have twitched ever so slightly. Maybe she wasn't so scary after all. Or maybe the unexpected show of support was just a trick of the light.

"Look, Remy. You can push Sheriff Holcomb only so far before he digs in his heels. Best to let him win this round."

Remy blinked. "You're offering me advice?"

"I'm offering you *good* advice. Golden. You'd be wise to take it."

Advice from Doris McCook was not to be ignored. The woman had been in Remy's life for as long as she could remember. As a close friend of the family, she'd attended her dance recitals, school graduations and just about every other special event in her life. The woman knew things about Remy, things others in town could only speculate about. As her brother Casey liked to say, "You can run from Doris McCook, but you cannot hide."

"Are you sure I pushed Wyatt too far?"

"I can think of one rather blatant clue." Doris looked pointedly at the closed office door.

Remy glanced over her own shoulder and frowned.

"Let him be." Doris patted her forearm in a surprisingly maternal gesture. "Save this particular fight for another day."

She could do that. But *should* she? That was the million-dollar question. Remy considered her options. Doris knew Wyatt as well as she knew Remy. She was probably right. Now wasn't the time to push him. Besides, Remy would see him again tomorrow. They would be on her turf. Out in the wide-open spaces, where no doors could be shut in her face. "You know what, Doris? I'm going to take your advice."

She would save the fight for another day.

Wyatt wouldn't know what hit him.

Chapter Six

Remy spent Saturday morning seeing a variety of patients. Nothing out of the ordinary, mostly cats and dogs brought in for their annual checkups. The only stressful encounter centered on her former high school chemistry teacher and her grossly overweight tuxedo cat. Weighing in at twenty-five pounds, the hefty feline needed to lose several pounds.

"Before you scold me," Mrs. Tumi warned in an anxious voice that said she knew she deserved a lecture, "I know Meeko Mouse needs to lose weight."

Remy kept silent. Shaming Mrs. Tumi wouldn't solve the giant kitty's weight problem.

"I don't understand why he keeps getting bigger. I took the bowls up off the floor, just like you told me. I'm measuring out his food. And yet, he hasn't shed a pound. Not one."

Mrs. Tumi was trying. Obviously not hard enough. Remy could interrogate the woman and probably discover that one cup was probably closer to two, plus treats.

"I love my boy," she said, dropping a kiss to his head. "I don't know what else to do."

"I'm going to give you a different cat food to try," Remy

said in what she hoped was an understanding tone. "It's a low-calorie variety that will make him feel full quicker than your current brand. I'll also take a blood sample so we can rule out any medical issues."

"You always were a smart girl. One of my favorite students after your sister."

Gritting her teeth at the backhanded compliment, Remy finished the exam. At the front desk, she gave Mrs. Tumi a two-week sample of the new cat food, then handed her off to Josh. The morning got busier after that.

Remy didn't pull onto her gravel drive until well after noon. She climbed out of her car and let out a sigh of contentment at she glanced over her personal sanctuary. She'd purchased the property and four-bedroom house five months ago. Exactly one month after her ugly breakup. Was any breakup not ugly?

Nothing had prepared Remy for the complete destruction of her relationship. She'd had such plans for her future, a loving husband, children of her own. Apparently God had different plans for her life. And so, Remy would trust the Lord. She would put her heart and mind and soul into a new dream, a new future and a new hope.

If she couldn't have children of her own, she would mold and shape young minds another way. Grasshopper Grange was only phase one. Remy needed much more land for her ultimate goal—a thousand-acre wildlife preserve and educational facility.

The private zoo on the neighboring property was exactly what Remy needed to launch her dream. Wildlife World had been mismanaged and was now facing bankruptcy. She would do better with the resources, once she secured a bank loan and made an offer to the current owners.

Soon, she promised herself. For now, she had to prepare

for Puppy School. She hurried toward the house. A series of low, throaty barks greeted her at the door. "There he is," she said as she stepped across the threshold. "There's my big boy. Miss me?"

Scooby's response included more barking and a wild, canine happy dance. "I missed you, too." She kissed his head.

Weighing in at 175 pounds and standing nearly thirty-two inches, Scooby was the perfect companion for a single woman living on the edge of town. When he stood on his hind legs, he was actually taller than Remy. His impressive size and deep, vicious-sounding bark scared off most predators. Assuming they didn't get too close. Scooby was the personification of a gentle giant.

He also thought he was a lapdog, which presented a few problems whenever Remy tried to read at night in her favorite chair. Scooby ran to the door and whined.

"Okay, okay. I get it. You need to go outside." She grabbed a fresh rawhide from the pantry, then opened the door and released the hound.

With surprising elegance and grace, Scooby trotted down the front steps and proceeded to do his business. "Good boy," she praised. "And here's your reward."

He took the rawhide with a polite clamp of his jaw.

The dog had barely settled on the porch with his treat when Brent's Jeep honked out a greeting. Older than Remy by only two years, Brent was her closest brother in age. After his five-year absence working overseas for Doctors Without Borders, they were still renewing their relationship. But things were progressing nicely, especially now that he was home for good, working as an anesthesiologist and raising his five-year-old twin daughters.

Remy adored her nieces. Harper and Kennedy were the reason she'd started the special Puppy School for young children. Recognizing Brent's Jeep, Scooby abandoned his chew toy and rushed to stand beside Remy. The dog loved the twins, but it was their six-month-old puppy that had stolen his heart, as evidenced by his excited barking.

Remy told the dog to heel. Perfectly obedient, he stayed glued to her side as Harper and Kennedy charged out of the vehicle. Kennedy held the puppy. Harper bounced along by her sister's side. "Hey, Aunt Remy," they said in unison.

Aunt Remy. Tenderness filled her. She had to swallow several times to release the air lodged in her throat. Brent had made a lot of missteps in the past, including a quickie Las Vegas wedding to a stranger. But God had turned his mistakes into two beautiful little blessings that called her Aunt Remy, just like her sister Quinn's daughters did. She loved her big family and desperately wanted to provide all of her nieces with more cousins to play with. But the odds were against her, and growing smaller as each day passed.

"Remy?" Brent's hand touched her arm, concern in his eyes. "You okay?"

"Never better." She shook herself out of her melancholy, then reached to take the puppy from Kennedy. Still in veterinarian mode, she said, "Let's have a look at our boy."

Sitting on the top step, she set Cooper on her lap. The potbelly had her quietly sighing. Apparently, today was the day for overweight animals. In this case, at least, the round belly was normal in a puppy Cooper's age and breed. He was a pug-mix with short, stumpy legs, a mostly tan body with a black face and ears, and the requisite smashed-in nose.

As if worried for his friend, Scooby placed his head on her knees and sniffed at Cooper. The puppy sniffed back. While he was distracted, Remy moved her hands over the animal's fur. She checked his spine, felt around under his belly. The puppy let out a loud burp.

Remy quickly set Cooper on a patch of grass at the bottom of the steps. The miniature pug spun around in circles.

Once finished, Cooper yipped, spun in another circle, then made a beeline for Scooby and instigated a wrestling match. The larger dog lowered to the ground and let his little friend crawl all over him, nipping along the way. While the animals roughhoused, Remy greeted her nieces properly, hugging first Harper, then Kennedy.

Harper was the first to pull away. "Watch me twirl like Cooper."

The little girl spun in fast circles. She stopped on a dime, then launched herself at Remy. Snuggling in, the child wrapped her arms around Remy's waist and squeezed. Breath caught in her throat, she lifted Harper in the air and then twirled her round and round and round.

Squealing in delight, Harper demanded, "Again, again."

Happy to oblige, Remy whirled her niece in another fast circle.

Kennedy begged for a turn. Remy put down one niece, then picked up the other.

"That was fun." Kennedy squirmed out of Remy's hold.

Back on terra firma, off she went, twirling in circles with her sister. The two laughed together as only little girls could.

"I remember you spinning around just like that at their age," Brent said.

"I don't know why I ever stopped." Remy had spent her childhood twirling wherever she felt the urge.

"You grew up."

"What a pity," she said, her eyes on the girls. Remy really wanted children of her own. But her recent endometriosis diagnosis had thrown a big wrench in her plans. Blinking away unwanted tears, she watched her brother watching his daughters. The man was smitten.

Would Remy ever know that sort of love, the love of a parent?

The sound of a purring engine drew her attention to the edge of her property as a familiar red Ford F-150 SuperCab steered onto the drive. Five seconds later, Wyatt pulled in beside Brent's Jeep. He took off his sunglasses and stared out through the windshield, his gaze intent, assessing, measuring, missing nothing. He caught sight of her, and his lips parted.

Remy wasn't fooled by that easygoing smile. Wyatt Holcomb was many things. Easygoing he was not. Several women in Thunder Ridge had their eye on the man. Remy would be lying if she didn't include herself in their number. She attributed her interest to the heady mix of the uniform, his loose-limbed confidence, those amazing eyes and the way he'd stepped up to take care of his nephew.

Gaze still locked with hers, he turned off the truck's engine and reached for the door handle, and Remy's mind emptied of all thought. Except one.

Here we go.

Wyatt held Remy's gaze as he pocketed his keys and prepared to exit his vehicle. He felt the usual punch of awareness whenever their eyes met. She was casually dressed today, in a pair of well-worn jeans and a fitted T-shirt that said You Either Like Animals or You're Wrong.

He smiled, thinking how much he liked her. The masculine interest felt wrong on many levels, especially with her brother standing right next to her. The same brother who had warned Wyatt to stay away from his baby sister years ago, one instance so intense they'd nearly come to blows. Well, Wyatt was a grown man now. And Remy wasn't a teenager. Brent could mind his own business.

"Can I get out now?" Samson asked from the back seat.

"Hang tight." By the time Wyatt exited the truck and opened the rear door, Samson was bouncing in the back seat, straining the laws of gravity despite the seat belt securing him in place.

Wyatt liked seeing the boy so excited. It didn't happen often enough, but more now that Remy was front and center in their lives. A lot had changed in the span of a few days.

"Be nice to the twins," he told the boy while helping him out of his seat belt.

Samson scowled. "I'm always nice, Uncle Wyatt."

"Except when you're putting frogs and lizards in Kennedy's cubby."

"I said I was sorry. Kennedy forgave me."

"Then you have a fresh start and that's always a good thing." Wyatt nearly added, "Don't blow it, kid," but decided that would only put his nephew on the defense.

Samson scrambled to the ground and took a good look around. "Wow! Is this where Miss Remy lives?"

Wyatt glanced at the tidy, single-story house with the wraparound porch. There was a lot of sturdy stone and wood and glass that should have seemed cold, and yet presented the image of a home rather than a house. "Yep, this is where she lives."

"I like it."

Wyatt did, too. Someone paid meticulous attention to the flower beds, adding the perfect blend of color and texture. He took care of the basic yard work at his own house. But, here, he could see himself really digging in. He would weed those flower beds, trim the bushes, lay out mulch. Maybe hang a tire swing. And…whoa. The image was a little too cozy.

"Hey, you two." Remy waved at them.

Samson spoke first. "Uncle Wyatt let me ride my bike all morning. It was super fun. I'm getting really good."

"I bet you are." She smiled at the boy, then switched her attention to Wyatt. "You're early."

He nodded. "I thought you could show me around the property before you start the puppy class."

"Not a bad idea." She placed a hand on each twin's shoulder. "I believe you know Harper and Kennedy."

Wyatt made a point of speaking to both girls, by name. He must have guessed right because Kennedy's eyes widened. "You can tell us apart?"

How to answer that without calling attention to the way his nephew couldn't meet the little girl's eyes? "Lucky guess."

This seemed to satisfy the child.

Wyatt greeted Brent next. They'd once been best friends, practically inseparable as boys. In high school they'd hung out with two other friends, Reno Miller and Brandon Stillwell. All four had left Thunder Ridge to explore the big world beyond their small town. All had come back, Wyatt first. Brandon next. Then Reno. Finally, Brent just six months ago.

"You're here for Puppy School?" Brent asked. "I didn't know you got a dog."

"We didn't."

"But I want one real bad," Samson added.

Wyatt sighed. "No dog."

"But, Uncle Wyatt—"

"I said no."

They went back and forth a few times after that.

It was Kennedy who rescued the situation. "You can play with our puppy. His name is Cooper."

Samson eyed the little girl tentatively. "Where is he?"

"He's over there with Scooby. Come on, I'll show you."

She took Samson's hand and pulled him to where a miniature dog was attempting to gnaw off another dog's massive ear. Remy's Great Dane, Wyatt presumed.

"I'll keep an eye on them," Remy said, following the children.

Brent broke the silence almost immediately. "How are you doing with—" Brent's eyes glanced over to Samson. "—you know. The whole parenting gig."

"Some days are better than others."

"Don't I know it." Brent stuffed his hands in his pockets and rocked back on his heels. "Anyway, I was thinking. Now that all the boys are back in town, we should fit in a hike sometime soon. Maybe next week, or the one after that? No kids, no women, just the guys."

Wyatt could use an afternoon with his old friends. It had been a long time since he'd hung out with just the guys. "I'll try to make it happen."

"Do or do not," Brent said. "There is no try."

Wyatt laughed at the quote from the sci-fi movie they'd watched a hundred times as kids. Yeah, he could use an afternoon with the old gang. "Text me the details. I'll make it work."

"Good man." Brent slapped him on the back.

Remy trotted back over. "Ready for the ten-cent tour?"

Wyatt hesitated, glanced over at Samson.

"I'll watch the kids," Brent offered. "What?" he asked his sister, mock insult in his tone. "I'm responsible."

Remy rolled her eyes, then indicated Wyatt to follow her. Once they were out of earshot of her brother, she started in on Wyatt. "So, about my permit—"

"Stop right there." He held up a hand between them. "I don't have any more information than I did yesterday afternoon."

She gave a short nod. "All right."

All right? Since when did Remy Evans ever give in that easily?

"We'll start here." She stopped at a small enclosure with waist-high fencing. "This is where visitors will interact with the animals. I'm thinking about adding concessions over there—" she indicated a spot on her left "—maybe a gift shop and a place for people to purchase additional animal feed."

Wyatt glanced around, trying to picture it, and liked what he saw.

"I'll put ducks in the pond over there." She pointed to a body of water too small to be called a lake. "Kids love feeding ducks. I'm also thinking about some wild turkeys and maybe some peacocks. Haven't decided yet."

"Sounds like you're putting together a pretty complicated operation."

She nodded, looking distracted. "I've already hired some part-time help. I'll need a social media presence. Possibly a webpage that lists the hours of operation and lots of candid pictures of the animals with kids. McCoy will help me with that. He's a good brother that way." She tapped her chin with her forefinger. "Maybe I'll send out a newsletter, too."

"You certainly think big."

She gave him a secretive smile. "You have no idea how big."

"Try me."

"I don't want to jinx it."

Not sure what that meant, Wyatt surveyed the network of fences, his gaze stopping at the pen where a familiar alpaca grazed. He moved closer for a better look. Prissy lifted her head. She made a happy, chattering sound, then trotted over to the railing.

Wyatt very slowly, very deliberately moved out of spitting distance. He could see Remy trying not to laugh.

"Hey, Remy. Wyatt." Brent waved them back to the house. "Work just pinged me. I gotta run in for an hour, maybe two. Can I leave the girls with you?" he asked his sister.

Remy patted her brother's arm. "You know you can."

"They come with Cooper."

She laughed. "You say that like it's a bad thing. Have you forgotten? I am the puppy whisperer."

"Right, my mistake. Work your magic, sis." He kissed his daughters goodbye, then pointed to Cooper. "Behave yourself." The puppy nipped his fingertip.

Shaking his head, Brent climbed into his SUV, then rolled down the window and pointed to Wyatt. "Next week. You, me, the boys. Don't even think about blowing us off."

"I'll be there." Once Brent pulled away, he went to his own truck and retrieved his tool belt from a compartment in the flatbed. He was strapping it to his waist, then paused when Remy hustled over. "What?"

"Nothing."

It was something. Her wide, rounded eyes were a dead giveaway. Wyatt let the silence hang between them and waited. People usually jumped right in. Not Remy. She was too busy staring at a spot just over his shoulder. "Remy, you want to explai—"

"Those latches won't fix themselves," she said, still looking over his shoulder. "Go on, now." She made a shooing motion with her hands, clearly wanting him gone. "Buh-bye."

Something was definitely off. Wyatt could feel it. Remy was extremely anxious, and he wasn't going anywhere until he figured out why. The flash of annoyance on her face only had him digging in his heels.

She made another shooing motion. "You're not leaving," she said with obvious impatience, eyes *still* not meeting his. "Why aren't you leaving?"

Wyatt could give her several reasons, starting with her very odd behavior. A gust of warm air stirred the hair just above his ear. It came again, warmer, a bit moist this time. He reached up to brush at the exposed skin. His fingers met warm, fuzzy flesh.

He spun around quickly. And found himself nose-to-nose with a startled alpaca.

"Prissy, no." Remy's warning only managed to agitate the already overwrought alpaca.

Wyatt moved a split second too late. Prissy did her thing. Then he was the proud owner of two ruined shirts.

Chapter Seven

Remy was genuinely glad Wyatt offered to take Prissy back to her pen without a single mention of dry-cleaning bills. Had he spoken about the incident, Remy might not have been able to keep from laughing. She did smile when Prissy, prancing alongside Wyatt as if they were old friends, leaned over and nuzzled his cheek. Wyatt froze midstep. But then, he gave the alpaca's neck an affectionate pat and kept moving.

Doris's words came back. *Sheriff Holcomb is a good man. One of the best I know.*

"Me, too," Remy whispered into the wind.

Parents began dropping off their children for Puppy School. Remy immediately hustled kids and puppies into the enclosure she'd cordoned off for the class. One final registrant had yet to arrive, the mayor's seven-year-old son. Remy's brother was also behind schedule. Since Casey was bringing extra puppies for her to use, she was forced to wait for him. That didn't mean she had to be patient about it.

She sent him a quick text. You're late, then added, You better be driving and thus unable to text me back.

She was stuffing her phone into her back pocket when

two vehicles turned into the drive. The first was a dark blue BMW sedan that Remy recognized as belonging to Thunder Ridge's newly elected mayor, Sutton Wentworth. Casey's ancient pickup of indeterminate age and color pulled in behind her. He owned two other vintage muscle cars he'd restored himself, but neither vehicle was suited for transporting puppies.

Casey exited the truck, circled around to the back and let down the tailgate. He reached inside a dog crate and pulled out two squirming bulldog puppies. Carrying one in each hand, he greeted the mayor and her son before passing one puppy to the boy and the other to Sutton. He was rewarded with a smile from the kid. He got nothing but a blank stare from Sutton.

Actually, no. That wasn't correct. The mayor looked unusually tense. Maybe it was because she was overdressed for anything to do with puppies. The black pencil skirt, high-heeled sandals and frilly lavender blouse were better suited for a boardroom or a television interview.

"Toby!" Samson shouted, waving frantically. "Toby! Over here!" Still waving, the little boy shot Remy a grin. "That's Toby. His mom's the mayor. He's my friend from school."

Toby said something to his mother. She responded with a nod. And then he was running in Samson's direction, puppy held tight against his chest. Casey was speaking to Sutton. She didn't respond, just looked down at her feet.

Shrugging, he went back to his truck, reached inside the crate and came out with one more squirming bundle of fur. He returned to Sutton's side. This time whatever he said had her laughing. Both smiling now, they began walking side by side, Sutton carrying one puppy, Casey holding the other.

Toby skidded to a stop in front of his friend. "Hi."

"Are you here for Puppy School, too?" Samson asked.

The other boy nodded. "My mom signed me up. Mr. Casey is letting me borrow one of his puppies. See?" Toby showed off the dog. "If I do good, I can maybe keep him forever."

Pure little-boy envy filled Samson's eyes. "Lucky."

There was a moment of chaos when Casey and Sutton arrived with their precious cargo. Remy took the puppy from Sutton first. "Thanks."

"You're welcome." Sutton smiled, then stepped back to stand next to Casey. The widow had undergone a remarkable transformation during the short journey from her car. There had been a brittleness about her when she'd first arrived, something frail and a little sad, more wounded bird than the tough city mayor she usually presented to the world.

Remy took the other puppy from Casey. His eyes narrowed at something in the distance. "Is that Wyatt out there by the animal pens?"

Remy told herself not to look. *Don't look.*

She looked.

The breath whooshed out of her lungs. Wyatt had rolled up his sleeves and was fiddling with the tool belt he'd strapped to his hips. He looked locked and loaded, a lawman to the core.

"That's him," she said, realizing Casey was waiting for her answer.

"What's he doing?"

"Fixing the latches on Prissy's pen."

Casey rubbed his chin between his thumb and forefinger. "Your alpaca get out and roam around town again?"

"I can neither confirm nor deny that."

"Uh-huh. I'll see if Wyatt needs any help." Casey spoke

low and quiet to Sutton, who actually blushed at whatever he said. Then her cell phone rang.

Sutton dug it out of her pocket and looked at the screen. Sighing, she lifted the phone to her ear and said, "This is Mayor Wentworth."

As she moved away, Harper tugged on Remy's arm. "I want to train Cooper this time."

"You got to train him last time," Kennedy said. "It's *my* turn."

Remy had prepared for this particular argument.

"Actually, I was hoping one of you would take charge of this little guy." She indicated the puppy in her right hand.

"Oh, he's cute," Kennedy said, always willing to be the peacemaker. "I'll take him."

Keeping the other puppy for herself, Remy organized the students in a horseshoe facing her, each with a puppy in their lap. "Our goal is to leave class today with a puppy that loves to listen."

She received several head bobs in response.

"Puppies have tiny bellies and short attention spans." As if to prove her point, Cooper decided to make a break for it.

Without missing a beat, Remy caught the puppy with her free hand, then continued her speech as she passed the animal back to Harper. "Today we're going to teach our puppies how to respond to their name."

Digging into her back pocket, she pulled out a plastic baggy filled with puppy treats. "We'll use a reward system to get them to respond. You'll say the name, then reward the dog. Say the name. Then reward. Name. Reward."

She demonstrated with her puppy.

"Now it's your turn."

The children worked on the technique for several minutes.

Next, Remy showed them how to wait for the puppy

to get distracted. "Then you hold a treat to their nose and guide the dog back to look at you. Say the name. Then reward."

She taught two more techniques, then checked her watch. The hour was almost over and parents were beginning to arrive to pick up their children. Sutton was still on her cell phone.

"Okay, we'll stop here. I want you to practice what we've learned this week at home. But before I let you go, I want to give you one final instruction. This is important, so pay attention." She waited for all heads to turn toward her. "Do not use your puppy's name this week unless you're training him or her."

"But how do we call them?" one of the children asked.

"You can say 'pup, pup, pup,' or use a general term like doggy, baby girl, baby boy, anything but their name. Got it?"

Nine tiny heads bobbed up and down.

Remy dismissed the class. Maybe the children would follow the rules. Maybe they wouldn't. The results would speak for themselves next week.

After escorting a mostly calm alpaca to her pen, Wyatt had returned to his truck to retrieve a fresh shirt, then spent the next few minutes getting his bearings. He then checked the variety of tools on his belt that had once belonged to his father. Before his death, Cyrus Holcomb had been a successful carpenter and handyman with a loyal customer base.

As a boy, Wyatt had loved following his father around at a worksite. He remembered graduating from handing the tools to his father to using them himself. It had been a rite of passage, as important in Wyatt's life as the decision to be baptized as a young adult. Samson would be old enough to assist Wyatt with odd jobs around the house soon.

Looking forward to that day, Wyatt studied the latch on Prissy's pen. It seemed to be in good working order. He would replace the entire mechanism anyway, and possibly add a padlock. He'd been considering what kind of locks when Casey arrived. "Want some help?"

Wyatt eyed Remy's older brother. The man had something on his mind, something that had put tension in his jaw. Wyatt had an idea what was coming and felt his own jaw tighten. "Depends."

"On what?"

Wyatt glanced at Remy, who was sitting cross-legged on the ground with a puppy in her lap. "If the offer is sincere, or you've come on a fishing expedition about your sister and me."

Looking very much like a big brother, Casey opened his mouth to speak.

Wyatt stopped him with a raised hand. "We aren't doing this again."

The other man didn't pretend to misunderstand. "No, we aren't."

Wyatt said nothing.

"My sister is a grown woman. It's none of my business who she dates."

"Remy and I aren't dating."

Casey didn't look convinced. "If you say so." Then Casey gripped his shoulder and squeezed. "The way I see it, my baby sister could do a lot worse than the town sheriff." He dropped his hand. "Amiright?"

Not even in the ballpark. Remy deserved a far better man than Wyatt would ever be. Casey knew this and had said as much once before. His other three brothers had given a variation of the same lecture, as had one other man. Ancient history. "Aren't you supposed to be asking me about my intentions?"

Casey grinned. "I never ask a question I already know the answer to."

So many ways to respond. Deciding silence was golden, Wyatt handed the other man a hammer. "Let's get to work."

"Wow, evasion," Casey said. "Subtle."

Wyatt preferred to call it self-preservation. "This is the pen I'm most worried about. Far as I can tell, Remy's alpaca has learned how to work the latch free." He hitched his chin in the direction where Prissy stood eyeballing them. "Our girl likes to roam around town eating geraniums out of flower boxes."

"So I've heard." Casey's eyes filled with amusement. "You gotta admire her ingenuity and commitment."

Wyatt had another name for Prissy's afternoon strolls through his town. "My association with this particular female has been wrought with nothing but trouble and aggravation." He thought about his spit-soaked shirt in the cab of his truck. "There will be serious consequences if she continues to mess with my attempts to preserve law and order."

"We still talking about the alpaca, or my sister?"

"Both. Either." Wyatt let out a humorless laugh. "You pick."

"I'd like to say it'll get better, but…" Casey trailed off into silence, dividing his attention between Wyatt and Remy. *"But,"* he repeated. "It's Remy we're talking about. My sister has always zigged when other people zagged."

That was one way of putting it.

Casey's humor turned into a thoughtful silence. "Thing is, despite the last time we had a similar discussion—"

"Discussion? That's what we're calling it now?"

Gaze averted, Casey studied the hammer in his palm, rolled it around a few times. "You got a better name for it?"

"You threatened me with bodily harm if I kissed her again." Memories of that day reared. Wyatt battled them back.

"Okay, yeah, I strongly advised you to stay away from her," Casey admitted without an ounce of remorse. "She was fifteen. And you were eighteen—"

"*Almost* eighteen." The distinction was important, legally speaking. And in several other ways, as well. None of which were important now.

"You also were about to leave for college, with no plans of returning. You'd made that clear to anyone who would listen. Despite what she told herself when she moved to Denver to be close to her jerk fiancé, Remy was always going to be a hometown girl."

Casey was right, about all of it. Remy had always dreamed of living happily ever after in Thunder Ridge. Wyatt had planned to shake the dust off his boots and never look back.

"Anyway, that's all in the past," Casey continued. "Truthfully, I think you'd be good for my sister, way better than that jerk Matt. But tread carefully, Wyatt. The breakup hit Remy really hard. Harder than I think most of my family realizes. Matt hurt her bad."

Wyatt hated thinking some man—*any man*—had hurt Remy, especially one she'd hoped to marry. Something dark and ugly moved through him. It took tremendous effort not to march over to where she sat and haul her into his arms. He wanted to soothe away her pain.

"That's my way of saying I hope things work out between you and Remy."

Wait— *What?* Had Wyatt heard Casey correctly? "Did you just give me permission to date your sister?"

"I'm not warning you off, if that's what you're asking."

It wasn't, but Wyatt's head was in a tailspin already. He wasn't sure how much more of this conversation he could take.

"You'll be happy to know, that's all I'm going to say on the subject." Casey gave Wyatt one final, assessing look, then turned to grin at Prissy. "What do you say we secure that wily beast standing over there posing as an innocent alpaca?"

"I say let's get to work."

Fifteen minutes after dismissing the children, Remy stood next to Wyatt. Both of them were silent as Casey executed a slow U-turn in her drive, then steered his ancient truck onto the road that led back to town. He was the last to leave, only a few minutes behind Sutton and her son, and barely fifteen minutes after Brent picked up the twins.

There'd been a moment of confusion when Samson and Toby begged to keep their puppies. Both Sutton and Wyatt had been firm in their refusal. However, Sutton's no came with a caveat that they would revisit the decision in three weeks when Puppy School ended. Wyatt hadn't given his nephew any such promise.

Remy understood. The man was busy, and still trying to find his way as a single parent. She glanced at him from out of the corner of her eye and tried not to laugh. "I see you changed your shirt."

"I keep a spare in my truck."

She did laugh then. "Aren't you the quintessential plan-ahead guy?"

To her surprise, Wyatt seemed to catch the humor of the situation. "A man never knows when he'll come across a startled alpaca."

They laughed together for several long seconds. Then both stopped.

There seemed to be a shift in the air. Remy had no name for the sensation turning her bones liquid. It was as if she'd fallen into some sort of new dimension where sound had scent, and sight had sound, and… What was happening?

Wyatt's eyes went very serious, as if he was battling his own shift in mood. Remy let out a shaky breath. It had been a long time since she'd felt this thrilled just standing next to a man, staring into his eyes. The air seemed to crackle between them.

"It's getting late," Wyatt said, his voice sounding low and a little hoarse. "Samson and I should get going…"

"Stay for dinner," she blurted out.

Wyatt blinked in surprise. "Really?"

"I'll wash your shirt while we eat."

His eyebrows slammed together. "You don't have to do that."

"It's the least I can do." One ruined shirt was bad enough. Two was completely unacceptable.

He seemed to contemplate her offer. "What's for dinner?"

Remy sucked in a breath. "An Evans family staple. Spaghetti and—"

"—meatballs. I remember." He looked about to say more, but Samson yelled from the porch, where he was petting Scooby.

"Can I throw the stick for Scooby?"

"Actually," Remy said, motioning the boy over, "I was thinking we could walk through the barn so you can get an idea of the sort of chores you'll be responsible for next week."

"I get to do chores? Cool."

"I like your enthusiasm, kid." Remy directed both Samson and Wyatt into the barn and introduced the animal in the first stall. "This is King Henry. He's a full-grown Shetland pony."

Samson eyes went wide. "He's so little."

And the perfect size for a seven-year-old boy. "You'll be taking care of him."

The boy's face fell. "I don't know how."

"That's not a problem." Remy reached down and rustled the already messy hair. "I'll show you how."

Samson seemed to think this over, looking very much like his uncle had when deciding if they would stay for dinner. Then, again like Wyatt, he smiled. "Okay."

Remy finished the abbreviated tour out back where her potbellied pig rooted around in the mud. "This is Horace."

"He kind of reminds me a little of my predecessor," Wyatt said, making Remy smile. The comparison wasn't too far off the mark. Sheriff Michaels had been rather squat and round in the middle. He'd also been a really nice man.

Samson tugged on her sleeve. "Didn't you say you have a ferret?"

"That's right, I do," she said. "Good memory."

The little boy looked around, frowning. "Where is he?"

"Farrell lives inside the house." She placed a hand on Samson's shoulder. "How about we head in there now?"

Wyatt's eyebrows lifted. "You named your ferret Farrell?"

"I like alliteration. Grasshopper Grange. Farrell the Ferret."

"Why not Grant the Great Dane? Alice the Alpaca?"

She made a clicking sound with her tongue. Leave it to Wyatt to miss the point. "That would be overkill."

"Right. Of course. My mistake."

The next hour was filled with a flurry of activity. Remy

started a load of laundry that included Wyatt's shirt, then fed her guests the promised spaghetti and meatballs.

Samson yawned over dessert. "Can I go play with Scooby and Farrell in the other room?"

"Sure."

The moment the boy disappeared, Wyatt said, "Thanks for feeding us. It was really great, even better than your mom's."

The compliment warmed her to her toes. "I enjoyed the company."

She didn't want the night to end.

"Let me help you with the dishes before Samson and I head out. You wash. I'll dry."

The offer was sincere, polite even. But Remy didn't want to wash dishes while Wyatt dried. It would be too intimate, something a husband and wife would do together. Add in Samson's laughter, Farrell's chattering and Scooby's happy barks, and the whole scene would feel too domestic, as if they were a real family. "Let's have coffee first."

"You sure you don't want to tackle the dishes before we relax?"

"Absolutely. Go sit with Samson. I'll bring the coffee out in a few minutes."

While the coffee brewed, Remy paced in a tight circle, trying to wrestle the nervous energy rushing through her veins into some semblance of order. What was happening to her?

Something big, she knew. Something that had to do with Wyatt. She took a peek into the living room, and regretted it immediately. Wyatt had settled in a chair facing the couch, his eyes on Samson. His expression was filled with the love a parent had for his child. Not uncle to nephew, but father to son. Remy thought her crazy, beating heart might crack a rib.

As if sensing her watching him, Wyatt turned his head and gave Remy a very different kind of smile. She scurried back into the kitchen, a lump the size of Montana lodged in her throat. What just happened?

She knew, of course. Everything had changed. For her, anyway. Nothing would ever be the same. She would remember this moment for the rest of her life. The moment when she fell forever in love with Wyatt Holcomb.

Chapter Eight

Wyatt couldn't shake the notion that something monumental had just occurred between him and Remy. One moment, he'd been holding her gaze. The next he was staring at empty air, his pulse roaring in his ears. That was intense, he thought, focusing on his surroundings instead of the way his breathing had become erratic. Or how his conversation with her brother earlier in the day had given him hope for a different future than the one he'd been facing yesterday.

There were splashes of color everywhere he turned his head, something he should have expected but oddly hadn't. Instead of being put off by the eclectic mash-up of styles and textures, he was immediately comforted. The room felt welcoming, homey even, and very, very Remy. He could see himself spending hours here. Samson on the floor playing with the animals. Another baby on Wyatt's knee.

He went hot, then cold, then spent the next few seconds watching his nephew move from the floor to the couch. The massive dog followed him. Shifting his big body in several different poses, he eventually wedged himself up against the boy. Samson was asleep within seconds, the Great Dane not much longer after that. Wyatt couldn't look at his nephew and not think of his sister, or how CiCi's self-destructive behavior had harmed Samson in ways he was still trying to understand. The boy needed his entire focus.

Wyatt covered his face with his hand, feeling guilt. Regret. A desire to do better. A high-pitched, chattering sound had him dropping his hand to search for the source. Farrell emerged from beneath a chair. The animal caught sight of Wyatt and squeaked excitedly. "Don't even think about it," he warned.

Pink nose twitching, Farrell's long, limber body arched gracefully across the floor.

"You're nothing but an overgrown rat." It was the pointy teeth, Wyatt decided. And the long whiskers. "Stay back."

Dark eyes glittered from behind the black mask of fur across the tan face. "I mean it. Not an inch closer."

In a lightning-quick move, the ferret slithered up his leg, across his chest, then wrapped himself around the back of Wyatt's neck. The animal's whole body went immediately limp in an impressive imitation of a feather boa.

Chuckling softly, Wyatt reached up and stroked the silky fur.

Remy entered the living room and blinked. "Huh." She set a steaming mug of coffee on the table next to Wyatt's elbow. "Farrell likes you."

"You sound surprised."

"I am. Farrell hates men."

Wyatt gave her a smug twist of his lips. "Not this man."

"Apparently not." Smiling now, Remy sat in the chair next to his and glanced over at Samson. "We wore the poor boy out."

"I should probably get him home."

"Drink your coffee first." Before he could argue, Remy went on the offense. "It's Saturday night. The boy is comfortable. Your shirt is still drying. Relax, Holcomb, and drink your coffee."

"What's a few more minutes?"

"That's the spirit. So…" She took a sip of coffee from her own mug and eyed him thoughtfully. "What's it like being the sheriff of Thunder Ridge? Run me through a day in the life."

Absently smoothing a hand over Farrell's silky fur, he thought about his answer. "No one day is like the other. I could be called out to investigate suspicious activity at a local business. Maybe monitor a traffic accident or resolve a domestic dispute." His least favorite. No good ever came from those calls. "I sometimes have to execute warrants. Break up a fight. And occasionally, if I'm really fortunate, I get to chase after runaway alpacas."

She laughed. "And here I thought you had a boring job."

"Actually, I do. Most of the time. Thunder Ridge is a peaceful community. The tourists that choose to come here are usually families and young married couples. The rowdier groups prefer the larger resorts."

Remy seemed to think that over. "Still," she said, setting down her mug on the tiny table between them. "It has to be a big change from your days playing professional football."

"Not that much different," he admitted, as surprised by his answer as she seemed to be. "I mean it. I was a quarterback. Both jobs require sound judgment, mental acuity and superior physical ability."

"Be serious, Wyatt."

"I am being serious. The skill set transferred really well."

She eyed him thoughtfully. "No regrets over quitting football and coming home? You were, what? Twenty-five at the time?"

"Just shy of twenty-four," he corrected.

"Still really young."

"Yeah." He'd been young. Young and selfish, and focused on pile driving through his goals. Play Division One football, earn a degree as a backup plan, get drafted into the NFL. He'd accomplished all of that by twenty-three.

Then the call had come.

"You were living the dream," she said softly, as if reading his mind. "And yet, you quit and came home."

"CiCi needed me."

"It was that simple?"

"She didn't handle my parents' deaths very well and I thought I could be a stabilizing influence in her shattered life." He'd been wrong.

Wyatt had been too young, and completely unprepared to take on an angry teenager. She'd fallen in with a bad crowd almost overnight. He hadn't been paying close enough attention. He'd been too focused on finding a new dream to replace his old one. At his sister's expense. He could admit that now.

"I failed CiCi," he said aloud, his voice rough with defeat.

"You didn't fail your sister, Wyatt." Remy's hand covered his. "You saved her."

He'd been telling himself that ever since he'd arrested her. "I'm not sure anymore."

"If you could go back in time, would you do anything differently?" Remy asked.

Wyatt had asked himself that question dozens of times, a hundred, always with the same answer. "I wouldn't change a thing."

Her smile, so full of acceptance and understanding, washed over him. In that moment, he felt at peace with the past. "Then you focus on that," she said. "And let God sort out the rest."

Deciding he'd had enough masculine attention, Farrell slithered down into Wyatt's lap, moved across his knees and then leaped into Remy's waiting arms. She cuddled the animal close and gave Wyatt another, softer smile. This one reached the darkest places in his heart and made him ache. He thought about following the animal's path— straight into Remy's comforting arms.

He woke up Samson instead. "Time to go home, little man. Before we overstay our welcome."

Remy arrived at her sister's house Sunday afternoon shortly after 1:00 p.m. She'd missed church, which wasn't typical but not unprecedented, either. She'd been forced to perform emergency surgery on a golden retriever that had been hit by a car just before dawn. It had been touch and go for a while, but the animal survived the surgery and was recovering nicely. Grace had promised to call Remy if his condition changed. At the moment, all looked good. The patient would live to chase squirrels another day.

Although she hated missing church, Remy was glad she was able to save a life and still make her family's weekly gathering at her sister's house. Quinn had taken over hosting Sunday dinner after their parents moved to Arizona.

Keeping with tradition, the guest list was never the same. On any given Sunday, Remy could expect an interesting and diverse mix of adults, children and an assortment of animals. Practically a member of the family in his own right, Wyatt had been attending since he was a boy. Now he brought Samson.

Remy pulled her SUV in beside his truck. Was she glad he was already here? Was she glad he was here at all? She wasn't sure. Her feelings for him felt new and raw and far more intense than when she'd been a teenager. His departure last night had been abrupt, leaving her wondering if his feelings for her would ever surpass the friendship phase.

She climbed out of her vehicle just as Casey's vintage 1963 red Ford Mustang pulled to a stop beside her. He hopped out of the driver's side and stretched his long legs as if working out invisible kinks. "Hey," he said.

"Hey back."

Stifling a yawn, he reached inside the car and pulled out his passenger. Winston was one of Casey's two English bulldogs. Winston's partner, Clementine, was probably at home running roughshod over her litter of puppies.

Remy hunched to the ground and greeted Winston with a kiss to his squashed-in snout. She caught a glimpse of Casey's face and stood up to face him. "You look like you've already put in a full day."

"Feels more like two." He rubbed a hand over his face. "I had to pick up a heart from a hospital in Denver and then get it back to Thunder Ridge for emergency surgery."

As a freelance cargo pilot, Casey knew how to fly all kinds of airplanes and helicopters. He was willing to brave any kind of weather to get the job done. Because of that, he was often contacted at odd times in the night when other pilots were either unavailable or refused to fly. "Did the patient survive?"

"He's in recovery as we speak." He yawned again. "I hope Quinn made chocolate cake. I could use a sugar rush."

Remy frowned. "Don't you own a coffee shop that serves homemade baked goods?"

"Nothing I sell comes close to Quinn's chocolate cake. If you tell Janelle I said that—" he pointed at her "—we are no longer siblings." Janelle was the pastry chef Casey kept on staff at Cargo Coffee. She was good. But not as good as Quinn. No one was as good as Quinn.

"Tell Janelle what?" Remy pretended complete and utter confusion. "I didn't hear you say anything about anything."

"You are officially my favorite sister."

"You say that now. But we both know you'll change your tune as soon as you get a piece of Quinn's chocolate cake."

"I plead the fifth."

Remy rolled her eyes.

He looked about to say more but seemed to change his mind. "Let's eat cake."

He whistled for Winston to follow. They entered the house to the sound of organized chaos. Children's laughter mingled with adult conversations. People milled about with plates overflowing with food. Craning her neck, Remy caught sight of Quinn's award-winning seven layers of chocolaty goodness on the sideboard.

Casey was on the move in the next instant, his "favorite sister" all but forgotten.

A familiar fat-bellied puppy came wheeling around the corner and dropped a large man's slipper at Remy's feet. "Nice job, Cooper," she praised the puppy. "You killed it dead."

He gave her a happy yip. Discovering a new delicacy, he began chewing on the toe of her shoe. "Bad dog." Trying to look stern, she picked up the puppy and held him up to her face. "No chewing on my new shoes."

"He's available for adoption." Brent came over, looking frustrated and overwhelmed. "Just say the word, sis, and he's yours."

"Your daughters would hate me for life."

"But *I* would love you for life. That animal is a menace."

"Cheer up. Once Cooper graduates from Puppy School, he'll be the best-behaved dog in the family. Won't you,

Cooper?" She snuggled the furry neck. "Won't you be a good boy after I'm through with you?"

Brent heaved a sigh.

"That being said—" Remy tucked the puppy under her arm like a football "—if he really does become too much for you, Brent, there's no shame in giving him away to a good home."

"He can come live with me," Samson said, peering into the room. "I mean, us," he amended, looking over his shoulder at his uncle.

"Who can come live with us?" Wyatt asked.

"Cooper." Samson shot out his arms to Remy. "Can I hold him?"

"No," Wyatt said at the same moment Remy handed over the dog. *Whoops.*

"Aw, he's so cute."

"We are not getting a puppy, Samson. I mean it. No dog. I don't have time to take care of an animal properly."

"That's okay, Uncle Wyatt. I'll do all the work."

"And that's how it starts," Brent said, clapping Wyatt on the back. "I said those exact same words. And look where that got me." He pointed to Cooper.

"I'm made of sterner stuff than you, Brent. Watch and learn." Wyatt gave the puppy a pat, then attempted to take him from his nephew.

Samson whipped around, presenting his back to Wyatt.

"Give me the dog, Samson," Wyatt said.

"No. I want to hold him a little longer."

It was Wyatt's turn to heave a sigh.

Brent snickered. "You are an oak, Wyatt. An immovable oak."

"I'm ignoring your sarcasm. No dog, Samson." This time, when he reached for the puppy he caught the boy off guard. "There." He passed the animal to Brent. "Done."

He might have been done, but Remy was not. She clicked her tongue and three more dogs appeared in the entryway, including Cooper's mother, Belle. Samson squealed in delight.

Brent howled with laughter.

"Stop undermining my authority," Wyatt ground out under his breath.

Remy ignored him. "Hey there, Belle." She picked up the full-grown pug-mix and tried to hand Cooper's mother over to Wyatt.

He went palms up in the universal sign of surrender.

"You know you want to hold her," Remy said, dangling the dog in the air between them.

"Doomed," Brent said to Wyatt. "You are so doomed, man."

Sighing, Wyatt took the pug. At the same moment, Samson asked, "Can I hold her next?"

"No." Wyatt glared at Remy as he carefully set Belle on the floor.

Taking pity on the man, she distracted Samson. "I think we need some cake right now. Come on, kiddo, the first slice is on me."

Samson dutifully followed her.

"I'm not going to forget this little episode," Wyatt called after her.

Remy waved a hand over her head.

"There will be a reckoning," he added.

Oh, Remy knew it. And, truthfully, she deserved a good scolding. She'd crossed a line. In her defense, Samson was a sweet kid desperate for attention. A puppy would help. A puppy would also add additional responsibility to Wyatt's already full load. Yep, Remy had definitely overstepped.

"I really want a puppy, Miss Remy. I mean, I know I

get to borrow one for Puppy School and everything, but it's not the same as having my own dog."

"I know, sweetie." But it wasn't up to Remy.

She was about to say something that would support Wyatt's stand, but Quinn entered the hallway. "Hey, Samson, just the boy I was looking for. I finished icing the vanilla cupcakes. I saved two for you." She leaned over. "I put them in our secret hiding place."

"All right!" Samson took off toward the back of the house.

"Secret hiding place?" Remy asked.

"That's between Samson and me." Quinn paused, looked hard at Remy. "You going to tell me what's wrong?"

What had her sister seen in her face? "I didn't say anything was wrong."

"You didn't have to. I'm older and wiser, remember?"

Oh, she remembered. All her life Remy had been compared with her *older and wiser* sister. Although they shared similar traits—there was no mistaking they were sisters—next to Quinn, Remy had always felt like the ugly duckling that never quite blossomed into a swan. Psychologists would say Remy had imposter syndrome. Or possibly a classic case of sibling rivalry. Remy just figured it was her lot in life. "I'm fine, Quinn."

Quinn's penetrating stare reminded Remy of their mother. It was a little off-putting. "You're absolutely sure you don't want to share anything with me?"

"I could use a giant piece of chocolate cake," she said. "And maybe a quiet place to sit and eat it."

"Don't you want lunch first?"

"One of the great things about being an adult is that I can eat dessert whenever I want." To demonstrate, Remy walked over to the sideboard and served herself a giant piece of cake. "I prefer to be alone when I indulge. You understand."

Quinn took the hint and left Remy alone. She found an empty seat in the living room and took her first bite. Pure bliss. She took another bite, closed her eyes and let the sugar rush wash over her.

Wyatt's deep voice washed over her, too. "You okay?"

Remy cracked open an eye. Her breath caught audibly at the look of affection on his face. The man had a really great face, especially when it was relaxed and smiling at her.

Still chewing, Remy took in his warm, sun-bronzed skin, the high cheekbones, the perfectly straight nose and the bold slash of dark auburn eyebrows that matched his hair color. She swallowed. "I owe you an apology."

"Yes. You do." He sat beside her on the overstuffed couch and tilted his head in anticipation. "Go on. I'm waiting."

"Oh. You want it *now*?"

"Now would be good."

Remy squared her shoulders, prepared to brazen her way through. She stumbled over her first attempt, sighed and tried again. "I'm sorry I undermined your authority with Samson."

"That could cover a lot of offenses, many of them in the last twenty-four hours."

Truth.

"How about you be more specific?" he suggested.

Wow, he was really making this difficult. Remy set her cake on a nearby table. She drew in a deep breath, huffed it out again. "I'm sorry I keep pressing the puppy issue. It's a massive overstep and I need to mind my own business."

"Was that so hard?"

Excruciating. "You have no idea."

"I applaud the effort. And—" he leaned in, eyes twin-

kling with satisfaction "—I accept your apology. Now…"
He cupped a hand under her chin and tipped her face up.
"It's my turn to apologize to you."

Say what? "Why?"

"For pushing back every time you try to do something
nice for my nephew. I know your heart is in the right place,
Remy. Thank you for being so good to Samson."

Her throat thickened at the affection she heard in his
voice, and the gratitude swimming in his eyes. "You're
welcome, Wyatt."

"Speaking of my nephew." Wyatt dropped his hand
and looked around the room. "Where did he run off to? I
thought he was with you."

"He is currently eating a vanilla cupcake Quinn made
special just for him."

Wyatt blinked in surprise. "Your sister made cupcakes
for Samson?"

"Well, sure. He prefers vanilla to chocolate." Remy
laughed. "Around this house that means he has few options for dessert."

"Your sister didn't need to go to extra trouble for the
boy."

"Of course she did. Samson is part of the family. Just
like you."

"Like…*me*?" There was raw vulnerability in the question. Wyatt was clearly baffled, as if he couldn't fully com-
prehend what was right in front of him. What had always
been right in front of him. He was one of them, as much a
part of the Evans clan as if he'd been born a member. Not
that Remy thought of this man as a brother. Or a cousin.

Now would be a good time for her to tell him how she
felt. But she wasn't ready. And, honestly, she didn't think
Wyatt was ready to hear what she had to say. A lot had

changed between them in a little over a week. But not enough.

Hoping to lighten the mood, she bumped shoulders with him. "Yeah, you big doofus. Samson is part of the Evans family, just like you."

He smiled, then. Not a smirk, not a mocking grin, a genuine smile that curled Remy's toes. She was helpless against the man when he looked at her like that. She did not want Wyatt Holcomb taking up residence in her heart. A still, small voice in her head said it was too late.

Too, too late.

Chapter Nine

The following morning, nerves nearly got the best of Remy. She wasn't sure what to expect when Wyatt dropped off Samson at her clinic. She'd rearranged her schedule so she could give the boy her undivided attention. Would Wyatt be all business? Would he joke with her? She had her answer when he dropped the boy off in a cold, oddly impersonal transaction. He hadn't been rude, more like... rushed.

Made sense. He was, after all, a busy man.

Deciding not to overthink his behavior, Remy showed Samson around the clinic. She introduced him to the staff, including the part-time tech home from college on summer break. "Your first job every morning will be to assist Jill." Remy made the introductions. "You two will feed and water the animals that have to spend the night with us."

Remy walked Samson through the process with the tech following along in silence. "You'll also help Jill walk the dogs."

"Can I play with them, too?"

"I certainly hope so." By 10:00 a.m. Remy was satisfied Samson understood his duties. Not only did he understand, he was bursting with excitement.

It took Remy no time to realize Samson was a bright kid with an active mind. He was also prone to boredom when he wasn't challenged or kept busy. She filed away the information for later. "Let's head out to the ranch now. We'll grab lunch on the way."

Out in the parking lot by her SUV, she took one look at Samson's battered sneakers and knew they wouldn't last a week. "Those won't do."

Samson looked down at his feet. "What's wrong with my shoes?"

"Not a thing," she said, thumping him lightly on the shoulder. "If you want to sit in my house all afternoon and read a book."

"Gross." His face twisted into a sour expression. "That would be awful."

"I know. So, let's get you the proper footwear before we head out to the ranch."

She took him to the Slippery Slope, a ski shop that catered to year-round outdoor activities, not just winter sports.

Seconds after entering the shop, Remy blinked hard, only mildly surprised when she saw a familiar auburn-haired man in a cop's uniform speaking to the store's owner, Reno Miller. Reno was a perpetual ski bum with the requisite lean, rangy build and spiky blond hair. He and Wyatt had been friends back in high school. They were still close all these years later.

Both had become professional athletes, although they'd chosen vastly different sports. Wyatt, football. Reno, downhill skiing, which had earned him several world championships and a few Olympic gold medals. The man had been a legend before he'd crashed, shattering both his shoulder and his career.

In the past six months, Remy had formed a solid friendship with the "Bad Boy of the Slopes," as one popular sports magazine had called him.

"Hey," Samson shouted. "It's Uncle Wyatt." The boy took off in Wyatt's direction. Remy followed at a more sedate pace.

"Hey, little man." Wyatt pulled Samson into a one-armed hug. "What brings you here?"

"Miss Remy is buying me a pair of boots just like hers. But for boys."

"He needs boots?" Wyatt asked, eyebrows raised.

"He can't muck out stalls in sneakers. Well, he could." She gave a little shrug. "But I don't recommend it."

"Makes sense." Wyatt reached for his wallet. Before Remy could stop him, he handed her several twenties. Normally, she would have said "keep your money," but she needed every extra penny to put toward the down payment on her loan. So she accepted the wad of bills with a nod.

Pocketing the money, she smiled at the other man. "Hey, Reno."

"Hey, girlie-girl. You're looking real good today." Reno gave her a quick once-over.

Reno was an outrageous flirt, harmless but very persistent. He never missed a chance to work his charms on Remy, with zero success, which only had him upping his game. It was really flattering. After her breakup with Matt, it was nice to know a man still found her attractive. Even if that man was nothing but a good friend. "Thanks," she said. "You're not looking too bad yourself."

Reno smacked shoulders with her. "Got any plans later tonight?"

"None that include you," Wyatt said, looking more than a little territorial as he nudged his friend away from Remy.

Was Wyatt jealous? Of Reno? That didn't seem possible. The two had never been attracted to the same woman.

Reno seemed equally surprised by Wyatt's response. "Dude, seriously? I was just asking an innocent question."

Wyatt shifted his stance, looking ready to rumble. "That so?"

"Yeah. Lighten up, man." Reno scowled at his friend, then made a grand show of winking at Remy. "We'll talk later, cutie-pie, when we can't be interrupted by a nosy lawman. In the meantime—" he clapped Samson on the shoulder "—how about we check out some kid-sized boots?"

As Reno steered Samson toward the back of the store, Wyatt watched the duo leave with a pensive frown on his handsome face. "Just how close are you and Reno?"

Something in his tone had Remy wondering if he was jealous. Or passing judgment. "We're friends."

He seemed to absorb her words, giving no indication whether he believed her or not. Then, he straightened, gave one firm nod and said, "He's a player, Remy. Be careful there."

"I'm a grown woman, Wyatt."

He said nothing.

"If Reno asked me out on a date—"

"I'd have to hurt him."

For several seconds, she stared at Wyatt, silent. He stared back, his eyes flashing with resolve. There was something else in his expression that unsettled her, a protectiveness that reminded her entirely too much of her brothers. "I'm not your little sister, Wyatt."

"I have never thought of you as a sister." He leaned in close, so close she could see the varying shades of green in his irises. "Not since I took you to prom."

More staring followed after this unexpected reminder of their one special night together.

He leaned in closer still. "You got me, Evans?"

No. Actually, she was more confused than ever. They never spoke of Wyatt's senior prom, or the humiliating day after when Remy had discovered her feelings for him were one-sided. The memory of his put-down—*you're not my type*—brought a fresh wave of embarrassment. And yet, she found herself saying, "I got you."

"Good." He shoved his hat on his head. "I'll pick up Samson by five. If I'm running late, I'll text you."

He left her staring after him.

This time, Remy didn't need to ask herself what just happened. She knew. Her heart had taken another hit. Any more of this, and she was going to need emergency triage.

The rest of the week proved relatively uneventful, which suited Remy just fine. She'd had enough of the drama between her and Wyatt. They fell into a comfortable rhythm, with Samson at the epicenter. There were no more tension-filled staring matches, no more pithy encounters over runaway alpacas, no more ruined shirts.

Wyatt dropped Samson at Remy's animal clinic every morning and picked him up at her ranch every afternoon. When she wasn't teaching Samson how to care for animals, she was providing him paper so he could continue designing his dream day care.

Remy's permit for Grasshopper Grange was approved late Tuesday afternoon. Wyatt gave her the news himself, having commandeered the certificate before Fiona had a chance to drop it in the mail. Pleased, Remy scheduled the grand opening a week from Saturday. By her calculation, she would have the money for the down payment on her loan before the end of July. She alerted her neighbors of her timeline, which suited their plans, as well. Life was good.

There was a minor incident with Farrell midweek. The ferret had managed to stow away in Wyatt's truck. How he accomplished this feat was a mystery. Although Remy had a few ideas. When the ferret repeated the same trick the next night, it became evident Samson was somehow involved. Wyatt was having none of it. He returned Farrell each morning, much to Samson's dismay. Poor kid. He really wanted a pet.

Remy decided to stay home Friday night and work on her website. She was uploading photos when her cell phone screeched out a song that indicated the caller was seriously "bad to the bone."

She scowled at the interruption. She'd assigned the ringtone to two people. Her brother Casey, a man who'd once been very much bad to the bone, or so the gossips claimed, and Wyatt. The song hit a crescendo. A picture of Wyatt from his football days appeared on the screen.

Remy checked the time before answering. What could the man possibly want at 9:00 p.m. on a Friday night? Equally curious, Scooby trotted over to stand beside her. "Might as well see what he wants."

With one hand rubbing the dog's head, she pressed the green icon and lifted the phone to her ear. "What can I do for you, Sheriff?"

He wasted no time getting to the point. "I need your help."

"Did Farrell become a stowaway again?" That was one determined little boy.

"I think Samson got the message." He sounded distracted. "I've been called into work."

"Don't you have deputies covering the evening hours?"

"This one's on me." Wyatt spoke in a calm, quiet manner, but everything in his strained tone said whatever needed his attention, it wasn't good.

"Can you come over and babysit Samson while I take care of the…situation?" He didn't expand. She hadn't expected him to. "Assuming you aren't on a date. Sorry, I should have asked first. Are you available?"

Of course she was available. On a Friday night. "I can probably make myself available."

"I'm desperate, Remy." He sounded harried and rushed. "I'll pay you for your trouble. Fifty bucks sound fair?"

"I'm insulted."

"A hundred dollars. Five hundred. Name your price. Anything."

The man really *was* desperate. "It's on the house."

He said nothing. Then, "I really appreciate this, Remy."

"Wyatt? Answer me one question. Was I your first or last choice?"

"You're my *only* choice."

"I'll be right over." She disconnected the call, shut down her laptop and then stuffed it in her tote bag. Scooby plopped his head in her lap and stared up at her, expectantly. "No, sweet boy, you cannot come with me."

He gave her his best puppy-dog eyes, no small feat from a giant, full-grown canine.

"I mean it. No." She'd already caved in to one male tonight. "No way. Wyatt won't like it. And Samson will be asleep."

Recognizing the name of his favorite little person, Scooby performed a fast spin.

"Still no."

Ten minutes later, Remy arrived at Wyatt's house, minus one very unhappy Great Dane. She'd make it up to him tomorrow, maybe with a jog around Thunder Ridge Lake. Scooby loved to run.

Wyatt answered her knock, looking official in his uniform. That was one big, bad-to-the-bone lawman.

She threw out her hands. "Here I am."

He didn't show any signs of relief, but his eyes warmed

as he stepped aside to let her inside the house. "Thanks for coming on such short notice."

"No problem." This was the first time she'd ever been in his home. Curious, she looked around, peeked into the kitchen, moved back to the entryway, frowned. The place was spotless. And way too neat for a single man with a seven-year-old boy. Actually, it was way too neat for any-one with a pulse. "You know, Wyatt, you could use a lit-tle clutter."

"What are you talking about?"

She swept her hand in an arc that included the hallway, living area and the rooms beyond. "You keep a remark-ably tidy house for a single dad."

"Don't be too impressed." His face was a mask of im-passivity. Impossible to read. And yet, Remy sensed she'd hit a raw spot with her words. "The housekeeper came today."

Remy made a scoffing sound. "Okay, sure, let's go with that."

"Remy." He took a step toward her, indecision in his gaze, as if he had more to say but wasn't quite sure how to voice it. And, oh, no, that was just too much man in-vading her personal space. She could smell him, and feel his heat, and...

"How long do you think you'll be gone?"

The question nudged him into action. "No idea." He grabbed a set of keys from a ceramic dish sitting on a small table. "Do you want me to text if this goes past midnight?"

"No need. I'm not going anywhere."

He showed her the big-screen television in the living room and walked her through how to use the universal re-mote. "Samson is already in bed."

Of course he was. Never let it be said Wyatt relaxed the rules, even on the weekends.

"He usually sleeps through the night."

Remy heard something in Wyatt's tone that had her asking, "But not always?"

"No." He looked toward the stairwell that led to the second floor. "Sometimes he has bad dreams."

Poor little boy. No wonder Samson had been acting out at school. The physical loss of his mother in the home had obviously left him scarred.

It had left Wyatt scarred, as well. Remy recognized the doubt in him, the guilt. After their conversation last weekend, she knew he wanted what was best for his sister and her son. Wyatt had big, broad shoulders, but he carried too many burdens for one man. He never complained, never spoke ill of his sister when he had every reason to do both. He really was a good guy.

On impulse, Remy laid a hand on his arm. "You're doing an amazing job with Samson. He's going to be fine."

"Thanks for saying that."

"It's the truth." The boy had Wyatt in his corner. It was really as simple as that.

"I really appreciate you coming over on such short notice," he said. "It was a big ask."

"I wouldn't want to be anywhere else." She meant every word.

They had one of their classic moments of silent staring. She couldn't look away. Wyatt seemed equally afflicted. But he surfaced first. "Text me if you need anything. Anything," he repeated, and then was gone.

Alone, Remy snooped around. She found nothing out of place, *nothing*, even the coasters on the coffee table that sat in a neat, precise, perfectly square stack. With a flick of her wrist, she scattered the entire pile across the freshly polished wood. Much better.

She checked on Samson. He looked so small cuddled

up in his bed, clutching a teddy bear. She returned to the living room, her eyes stinging. Picking up the remote, she sank onto the sofa and grinned. Well, well. Wyatt might keep a spotless house, but his furniture was big and squishy and really, really comfortable. He also had state-of-the-art electronics and a subscription to every streaming service known to man. "Aren't you full of surprises, Sheriff."

Wrapped in plush coziness, Remy leaned her head back and went channel surfing.

She could get used to this.

Chapter Ten

Several minutes after midnight, Wyatt pulled into his driveway, cut the engine of his cruiser and sat looking out into the dark. His mood landed somewhere past furious. It had taken him and two of his full-time deputies the better part of three hours to process the dozen underage drinkers with Minor in Possession charges, then contact their parents and explain next steps.

The good times hadn't stopped there. Oh, no. Two of the teenagers, both repeat offenders, had become downright chatty when they realized the misdemeanor would stay on their record for a year, and thereby jeopardize their college scholarships. They'd ratted out the parents of the party's host, who'd provided the alcohol.

When Wyatt had pressed the unrepentant couple for an explanation, he'd gotten a whopper of an excuse. "Hey," the father had said with a shrug, "kids are going to drink anyway, might as well make sure it's in a safe and controlled environment."

Wyatt had blinked at the man.

"I mean," his wife added, "how much trouble can they get into at our house?"

"You served alcohol to minors," Wyatt had told them. "No getting around it, you broke the law."

They'd lawyered up at that point. Wyatt had charged them with a Class 2 misdemeanor and left the rest of the processing up to his night deputy. Josh was the father of three teenagers and more than happy to take on the responsibility. Messy business all around.

Wyatt exited his vehicle and stepped into the still night air, his mind on the days when he'd had a teenager in his house. Adolescence was a minefield filled with academic and social pressures. Add in hormones and the desperate need to fit in, and bad things were bound to happen. It was up to parents or, in his case, guardian to guide their teenagers through the rough patches. Supplying alcohol was never the answer.

Too tired to think about the rest, he entered his house. A blissful moment of peace filled him. He liked the idea of coming home to Remy, liked knowing he was steps away from receiving one of her gorgeous smiles.

She'd turned down the lights in the living room. The soft hum of the television played in the background. He stepped deeper into the room and looked around. He didn't see Remy at first. Then he did. She was curled up on the sofa, looking soft and feminine and his. *Mine.* The thought came so fast it threw Wyatt back a step. He forced himself to move closer.

A strand of hair had fallen over her cheek, a black satin ribbon against pale, pale skin. Tenderness moved through him. He had to roll his shoulders to dislodge the sensation.

He needed to wake her up. He watched her a second longer, feeling somehow cleansed by her presence in his house. This was Remy. *His* Remy. Cuddled on his sofa, her head resting on her bunched hands. She took his breath away.

Maybe he should let her sleep. He could go back to

the jail, finish up what he left in his deputy's hands. Josh wouldn't appreciate his return. The man had relished the responsibility Wyatt had given him.

Besides, if Remy's brothers found out she'd spent the night in Wyatt's house, no matter how innocent, they would come after him again. The same way they had the day after prom. One by one, they'd warned him away from Remy.

The years fell away and he was seventeen again, discovering he had feelings for her. Real feelings, the kind that lasted a lifetime. He'd stood his ground with each of her brothers.

They'd overstepped, plain and simple. But they'd also been right. Remy had been too young. And he'd had one foot already out of Thunder Ridge. Had he pursued her back then, he would have broken her heart. His own heart wouldn't have fared much better.

But he was a grown man now. And Remy was a grown woman. There was nothing keeping them apart. Except everything. Wyatt had focused too much on his own life once before, building his name in the sheriff's office, his eye on the position he had today. CiCi had paid the price. Wyatt wouldn't make that same mistake with her son. No distractions.

That didn't mean it was easy for him to keep away from Remy. She was light and joy and everything good. And Wyatt wanted to lean into the comfort of just being in her presence. At least she snored. Instead of irritating him, the soft, delicate sound made him smile.

Oh, man, he had it bad. He reached out and touched her cheek. "Remy," he whispered. "Wake up, sweetheart."

She sighed softly. The sound nearly brought him to his knees.

"Come on. Wake up."

Her eyelids slowly opened, fluttered shut, then snapped open again. "Wyatt!"

He smiled down at her. "Hey."

"Hey." She rubbed at her eyes. "What time is it?"

"After midnight."

"That late?" She leaped to her feet, her head missing Wyatt's chin by a centimeter. His natural reflexes had saved them both from a lot of pain. A definite metaphor for their relationship. "I better get home," she said, looking around with wide, confused, sleepy eyes.

"Are you okay to drive?" he asked. He could call one of his deputies to drive her home.

"Why wouldn't I be okay to drive?" Remy spun around to glare at him, eyes perfectly clear. "Hey, you look wiped out. That must have been some call."

"Pretty bad."

Her hand came to rest on his forearm. "Can you tell me about it?"

"Not really, except to say it involved teenagers, irresponsible parents and a lot of bad judgment on everyone's part."

"And now you're thinking about CiCi."

Wyatt *really* didn't want to have this conversation. "Yeah, I am."

"Arresting your own sister must have been unbelievably difficult."

"Worst moment of my life."

Which was saying a lot. Wyatt had been forced to quit his dream job, take on a new one, all of this after burying his parents. Each event had been harder than the one before, but nothing compared to hauling his sister to jail.

"Do you regret arresting her?" There was understanding in Remy's voice, and Wyatt felt a crack in his heart opening to her. She'd always been able to get past his defenses.

Even in high school, she'd pushed past the cocky jock, straight to the boy with hopes and dreams and fears that he'd fall short against football players from bigger cities.

"I regret a lot of things, but no. Not that," he admitted. "I'm a lawman to the bone, even when it's hard. I can't see myself doing anything else. I like being the sheriff of a sleepy little Colorado town. That being said, some-times—" like tonight "—I wouldn't mind having no other responsibility than executing a perfect spiral straight into the hands of a world-class wide receiver."

She nodded, then moved a step closer, her face soften-ing. "You traded all that fun and glory for your sister. I can't imagine the decision was an easy one."

Easier than he'd expected. Of course, playing ball had never been about the trappings. It had been pure love of the game. "I don't miss the fame or the big city or the cushy lifestyle I left behind. Thunder Ridge is my home. It's where I belong."

"But…"

"I miss the purity of the game. I would be lying if I said otherwise." Just saying the words made his fingers itch to hold a football. "There are moments when my mind wants to look back, and wonder 'what-if,' but then something happens at work, good or bad, and I realize how fortunate I am to serve the citizens of Thunder Ridge."

Remy took his hand, pulled him close and pressed her cheek on his arm. "You're a good man, Wyatt Holcomb."

Exhaustion took over. Needing to lean into the com-fort she offered, he moved quickly and wrapped her in his embrace. "Sometimes, like tonight, I feel like I'm bat-tling smoke."

"I have days like that." Sighing, she put her hand in the center of his chest and stared at her fingers. He could feel his heart beating furiously against her palm.

He went very still, willing Remy to look up at him. Silently begging her to keep staring at her hand. The conflicting wishes only added to his struggle to do the right thing and set her away from him.

A beat passed, two. Finally, she lifted her head. The low light gave her skin a golden tint and highlighted the shiny black layers of her hair. Her beauty stole his breath. The mix of concern and affection in her eyes had him leaning down. Closer, until his lips rested against hers. The kiss lasted two seconds, maybe three. He pulled away with a start.

What was he doing? She'd been offering him comfort and he'd taken advantage of her kindness. He shook his head slightly, holding her gaze, overcome with remorse. "I'm sorr—"

"Don't." Her fingertips pressed against his mouth. "Don't apologize. Anything but that."

"I wasn't going to apologize." Except that, yes, that's exactly what he'd been about to do.

Worse, he longed to drag her back into his arms for a real kiss. He didn't do it. His sole focus had to be on Samson. He owed that to CiCi.

"It's been a long night for both of us. You'll want to be getting home now," he said, taking her arm by the elbow. "I'll walk you out."

As Wyatt held on to her elbow with a firm yet gentle grip, Remy swallowed against the biting pressure welling in her throat. Her eyes wanted to fill with tears. But no. She would not cry. Not in front of him. Not again. Once in a lifetime was enough.

"Stop walking so fast," she protested, tugging on her arm. He moved faster.

Disoriented, robbed of her equilibrium, Remy struggled to keep up with his quick, purposeful strides. It was the worst feeling, not knowing what was going on in Wyatt's mind. He seemed completely unaffected by their kiss.

That couldn't be true. He'd kissed her. And with such tenderness. The gesture had been really, really sweet and surprisingly intimate for something that had lasted only a few seconds.

And yet, here they were, back in a familiar place. Back to Wyatt dismissing her, walking her out of his house at a fast, steady, no-nonsense pace.

Why did he keep pulling away when things were just starting to get good?

The feelings between them were real. She knew it. He knew it—how could he not? Something was emerging between them. Stronger than before, potentially life-altering. Did Wyatt acknowledge any of this? Nope. His first instinct was to apologize, which proved he still thought of her as his best friend's little sister instead of a full-grown woman who'd experienced her own share of setbacks.

Not that he'd ever asked her about her life, or her disappointments, or even her hopes and dreams. He'd yet to bring up Matt. Wasn't he the tiniest bit curious about her breakup? Apparently not tonight. He was too busy perpwalking her out of his house. Okay, maybe perp-walk was a slight exaggeration.

Mouth grim, he opened the front door and stepped out onto the stoop, pulling her along. The world around them was nothing but moonlight and shadows. And would have been romantic if Wyatt wasn't looking so resolute and bleak. She sighed.

"It's late," he said. "And I woke you from a sound sleep." He swung around, his gaze searching her face. "Are you sure you don't want me to call one of my deputies to take you home?"

The concern was pure Wyatt. He was a protector, always had been. Even when he'd broken her heart, he'd done it as gently as a seventeen-year-old boy was capable. His words had been brutal but had lacked condemnation. She knew that now, could admit the truth. With time and distance she had clarity. Some days Remy really hated being a mature adult.

"No need to worry about me," she said. "I'm wide awake."

"Text me when you get home, okay?"

She nodded. "Sure."

"Thanks again for coming over tonight." He let go of her arm and gazed down at her with what could be described only as focused yearning, as if he was collecting memories of her.

Oh, Wyatt. She reached up to touch his face. The scratchy feel of his unshaven cheek against her palm filled her with affection. Remy was starting to feel slightly desperate. For what, she didn't know. She lifted onto her toes and pressed her mouth to his.

His breath caught.

They blinked at one another. Then both stepped back.

"Remy, I… That is…" His words trailed off into a masculine growl of impatience. He seemed taken off guard. It was gratifying to know she wasn't the only one in a state of confusion over a kiss—*two* kisses, really.

"I suppose I should be going," she said to fill the awkward silence. She climbed into her SUV and reached out for the door. Wyatt caught hold of it first.

One arm on the door, the other on the hood of the vehicle, he leaned in until their faces were level. They hovered in silence for a full five seconds. Remy counted. Beyond that, her mind couldn't form coherent thought. It was difficult to wrap her brain around the fact that he'd kissed her tonight. And then she'd kissed him. Would one of them go for a third?

Remy had her answer when Wyatt stood to his full height, and said, "Don't forget to text me when you get home."

She swallowed back a sigh. "Okay."

"Good night, Remy."

"Night, Wyatt."

It took her the entire drive home to compose the text she would send. No, make that two texts. Only once she was settled on her sofa did she type out the first. I'm home.

Before she lost her nerve, and while the dancing bubbles played beneath her message, she sent the second text. I'm not sorry we kissed.

Wyatt's response came five full seconds later. I'm not sorry, either.

Remy stared at her phone. Was Wyatt finally coming to see her as a grown woman? His kiss said yes. Would he act on his feelings? His behavior after his kiss said no. And that, Remy decided, put them back at square one. Story of her life. At least, where Wyatt was concerned.

Chapter Eleven

Remy woke the next morning to a bright Colorado sky and another text from Wyatt. Any chance I can drop off Samson an hour early for Puppy School?

She read the text twice before answering. Trouble in Dodge City?

Just a few details that need tying up. Shouldn't take long.

She tried to read between the lines. Last night he'd mentioned teenagers and irresponsible parents. Remy's heart squeezed with worry. She prayed no one had been hurt. Drop him off at the clinic any time before noon.

When Wyatt showed up ten minutes before the deadline, he was dressed in regular clothes. He'd paired dark jeans with a light green long-sleeve button-down dress shirt. He looked good in business-casual clothing. He also looked exhausted. "You get any sleep last night?" she asked him.

The question earned her a ghost of a smile. "A couple hours."

"I slept really well," Samson told her, wrapping his arms around her waist in a fierce hug.

She held on to him tight for several seconds, wishing

she never had to let go. She was really starting to care for this kid. "That makes two of us."

Samson grinned up at her as he shuffled out of her arms. "I can't wait for Puppy School today. Do I get to train Roscoe again?"

Remy had to think, then remembered that was the name he'd given the puppy Casey had loaned him for class last week. "I don't see why not. You did such a nice job with him last time."

"I really like Roscoe. I should maybe practice with him this week." He spared his uncle a quick, hopeful glance. "Puppies learn best when they practice."

Wyatt didn't respond. Remy thought maybe she detected a slight exhalation. His version of a sigh. "I better get moving." He slid Remy a look. "I'll try to get out to your ranch by three."

"Whatever works."

He didn't say anything, just pulled his sunglasses out of his front pocket and placed them on his face, the move hiding his eyes. "Don't you have *stuff* to do for the party tonight?"

"What party?" Samson asked before she could answer.

"My family and a bunch of our friends are getting together to celebrate my brother's engagement. He's marrying Harper and Kennedy's aunt Hope."

Samson seemed to think that over, then said, "Do I get to come, too?"

"I'm pretty sure you were invited." She glanced at Wyatt for confirmation. "Right?"

"We were invited."

She arched a brow. "And…?"

"And—" he gave her a small smile "—we'll be there."

Samson's excited whoop spoke for itself.

It became clear on the drive out to Remy's ranch that

Wyatt hadn't told the boy about the party. Typical man, she thought. Samson had a million questions. He wanted to know who would be at the party. What kind of food they would be eating. "Will we get to play games?"

"I'm sure there will be lots of outdoor games," she said, "Volleyball, for sure." This seemed to satisfy him.

The next few hours went by in a blur. At Puppy School, Remy taught the children how to lure the puppies around with no commands, just food. "This way they learn how to associate obedience with positive rewards."

They learned how to use playtime to teach the animals the words *out* and *sit*. She wrapped up the session with lots of time to practice the new skills. Samson sat next to Toby and followed Remy's instructions to the letter. He played nice with Harper and Kennedy, and was generally a perfect little boy, which Remy made sure to tell Wyatt when he arrived a few minutes after she dismissed Puppy School. His eyes narrowed. "Nice try. He's still not getting a puppy."

Remy shivered at the intense look on Wyatt's face, a man hanging by a thread. Now was definitely not the time to push. "That's between you and your nephew."

"Exactly."

She let out a shaky breath. "I guess I'll see you tonight, then?"

"Guess so."

Two hours later, Remy walked into her sister's house wearing a blue floral sundress, her favorite summer sandals and a smile. She'd made sure to arrive before the official start of the party, in case her sister needed help. Now that their parents lived in Arizona, Quinn not only hosted Sunday gatherings but all of their family get-togethers in Thunder Ridge. Tonight's celebration was no exception.

Remy's contribution was a dozen bags of chips and

half that many dips. She wasn't especially gifted in the kitchen like her sister. Quinn owned a successful shop in town that served every kind of chocolate treat imaginable, often made by her own hands.

Remy could barely boil water.

She went to deposit the chips and dips in the kitchen. She found the soon-to-be husband and wife alone. And kissing. "Sorry." Remy backpedaled. "Didn't mean to intrude."

The happy couple broke apart, laughing. "You weren't intruding," Walker said, still staring into his future wife's eyes. "Much."

Wow, that look on her brother's face. Remy had despaired of ever seeing Walker love a woman that fully, that completely again. After losing his wife and unborn child to a series of medical complications, he'd buried himself in work. But then Hope had come looking for the twins' father and everything had changed for Walker. For Hope. For them all.

Hope shifted out of Walker's arms and approached Remy. The happiness in her gaze mirrored the one on her fiancé's face. "Let me take those for you."

"Thanks." Remy passed over the grocery bags and looked around the empty kitchen. "Where is everybody?"

"Quinn ran to her shop for more cupcakes," Hope said, rooting around in the bags. "She took Skylar and Sinclair with her." *Too bad*, Remy thought. She would have liked to hang out with her nieces before the party got rolling. "Casey and McCoy are outside setting up the volleyball net. Brent is running late with the twins, something to do with a wardrobe crisis." Hope turned to Walker. "Who else am I missing?"

"Grant went out for more ice." Poor guy. Quinn's husband was always stuck with that thankless job.

"That's right," Hope said. "Grant went out for more ice." She smiled at Walker.

He smiled back.

They got lost in each other's gazes and Remy hightailed it out of the room. She was happy her brother had found love a second time. No, really, she was. But Remy couldn't stop herself from thinking about her own situation. Six months ago, she'd been planning her own engagement party. Would others have the same thought? Would they look at her with pity tonight? Whisper behind her back?

It wouldn't be the first time.

The front door swung open. Her nieces rushed into the house, Brent several steps behind. The poor guy looked like a worn suit fraying at the edges. The twins, on the other hand, couldn't be more adorable. They wore matching yellow sundresses with pretty white daisies. Their hair was pulled back in sleek ponytails, the only hairstyle Brent could manage thanks to Remy's patient instruction.

She greeted her nieces. Guests started arriving soon after that. Remy knew the exact moment Wyatt stepped across the threshold. Her heart switched from a slow, even thump to dancing a merry jig against her ribs.

"Miss Remy." Samson shot in her direction. "I rode my bike again today."

"Fun." She hugged the boy close. "The other kids are out in the backyard."

Samson ran back to his uncle. "Can I go outside?"

Wyatt nodded. "Have fun."

The little boy didn't have to be told twice.

Wyatt continued in Remy's direction in that smooth, even gait that was so much a part of him. He was wearing the same clothes he'd had on earlier in the day. He hadn't shaved, either. Stubble darkened his jaw, making him appear a little dangerous. His hair was slightly disheveled, too, as if he'd shoved his hands through it more than once.

He looked good, really good. Helpless against the pull of him, she watched his approach.

He's not here for you. She told herself this, repeated it several times, but her heart still skipped several beats. He had that look in his eyes. The one that had stared at her right before he'd kissed her.

Had that been only last night?

Wyatt stopped a few feet in front of her. He looked solemn and maybe a little nervous, his gaze darting around the room. It wasn't the first time she'd noticed the way he checked his surroundings. Was that what came from being a lawman, that constant gauging and measuring, looking for danger even in a friend's home?

Thunder Ridge was a safe town. Mostly thanks to him and his competent leadership in the sheriff's office. Remy had never really thought what that must cost him.

"Hey," he said.

"Hey." What was wrong with her? She was usually a lot chattier than this. Wyatt was a man, and a flawed one at that. His eyes looked tired. "Long afternoon?"

"No worse than usual."

There it was, her chance to broach the subject that had been on her mind since last night. "Seems you get pulled in a lot of directions."

"I knew what I was signing up for. At least, at work. At home?" He glanced in the direction Samson had taken through the house. "I'm still finding my way."

"Maybe I can ease your mind where Samson is concerned." She waited for him to look at her again. "How about we make our temporary arrangement permanent?"

"Permanent?" He looked startled by the offer, like that

was the last thing he expected her to say. "You realize school is out of session through the middle of August."

"I know." This was vital information if she wanted to open her wildlife preserve and educational facility in time for the new school year. "It's no hardship, Wyatt. I like Samson. He likes me. We've found a rhythm that works. Why put the boy into another situation when it isn't necessary?"

Wyatt didn't answer right away. But she could see the wheels were spinning. A lot was going on in the man's head, and Remy wasn't entirely sure all of it had to do with his nephew. "You make several valid points."

"Is there any other kind? No." She shot up a hand to keep him from speaking. "Don't answer that. I already know what you're going to say."

"What's that?"

"You were going to say—" she pitched her voice to a lower octave "—'Thank you, Remy. Samson will be in good hands with you.' Go on, Wyatt, say it."

"Thank you, Remy. Samson will be in good hands with you."

"Was that so hard?" she asked, using his own words against him.

"Not even a little." He cleared his throat. "While I have your attention. We should probably discuss—" The rest of his words were cut off by the buzz of his cell phone. "Hang on."

He took one look at the screen, blew out a mild hiss of frustration, then shoved the phone in his back pocket. Annoyance etched his features.

"Problem?" she asked.

He nodded. "Work."

"It's been a busy few days for you."

"It's not usually like this." He sounded baffled. "Actu-

ally, it's never like this. Must be something in the water."
He circled his gaze around the room, looking distracted,
slightly worried.

Remy touched his arm. "Go to work, Wyatt. I'll keep
an eye on Samson until you get back."

"This will be the third time in two days you've helped
me out of a jam."

"I don't mind." It felt good to be needed, especially by
this man. "Go, Wyatt. I've got things covered here."

"I promise to make it up to you."

She touched his arm. "Don't think I won't hold you to
that."

He left the house shaking his head.

Wyatt walked out of the jail two hours after arresting
Harley Durham for knocking his wife around. It wasn't
the first night he'd been called out to the Durham home.
Harley had resisted arrest. Wyatt had been faster than the
man's flying fists. When she saw her husband in hand-
cuffs, Suzie immediately began changing her tune. Wyatt
had hauled Harley off to jail anyway. Then he'd contacted
the couple's pastor. Brandon Stillwell immediately left the
party at Quinn's to counsel Suzie.

Before climbing into his truck, Wyatt texted Remy to let
her know he was finished up and heading back to Quinn's.
She sent him a thumbs-up emoji, followed by two hearts,
then three miniature alpacas. He was still smiling when
he pulled into Quinn's driveway five minutes later.

There were considerably fewer cars than when he left,
with the exception of the typical stragglers. Mostly mem-
bers of the Evans family. And Reno. Wyatt recognized
his friend's Jeep, an even older model than the one Brent
drove.

Wyatt was met at the door by Samson. The boy had a

very serious expression on his face. "Okay. It's like this. The house was really messy." He made a karate-chop motion with his hands. "But I helped clean up."

For several seconds, Wyatt stared at the boy in muted shock. It was a battle to get Samson to put his clothes in the hamper. One week with Remy and he was a different kid. "Sounds like you had fun tonight."

"The best time ever."

"Where is Miss Remy?"

"Washing dishes." Samson spun around. "I gotta get back to my job. I'm in charge of folding blankets." He took off for parts unknown in the house, presumably wherever "folding blankets" took place.

Wyatt found Remy in the kitchen. She was not alone. While she washed, Reno dried. Standing together at the sink, they looked entirely too cozy. Remy's dark hair stood in stark contrast to Reno's blond streaks. Once considered a bad influence by Wyatt's own father, and not always a favorite among the town gossips, Reno had executed a huge transformation in the past five years. He was now a well-respected citizen of Thunder Ridge. The quintessential hometown boy made good.

Wyatt liked Reno. He considered the man a good friend, one of his closest. At the moment, he was standing entirely too close to Remy, looking far too chummy as they stood shoulder-to-shoulder at the sink.

Remy said something low and husky to Reno. Laughing, he reached his hand in the sink and flicked soapy water at her. Wyatt saw red. The former pro skier may have turned his life around. But Remy was still too good for him.

The shot to Wyatt's heart was not jealousy. It was concern for a friend. Remy been through enough. She didn't need another heartbreak, especially not via the "Bad Boy of the Slopes."

Wyatt cleared his throat. Twice.

The two glanced over their shoulders at him. Reno shot him a smug grin. Remy's expression was harder to interpret. "Sorry to interrupt all the fun." He hadn't planned to sound so sarcastic or surly. He blamed his foul mood on Harley Durham.

Still grinning, Reno turned completely around to face Wyatt head-on. "Dude." He continued drying the plate in his hand. "You look terrible. Like maybe you need to get some sleep."

"Yeah, maybe." Wyatt could do without the running commentary from the peanut gallery.

"Everything turned out okay?" Remy asked.

He nodded.

"That's good to know."

He cleared his throat again. "Sorry it took me so long to wrap things up. Looks like I missed most of the party."

"You're here now," she said. "That's what matters."

"Did Samson give you any trouble?"

"Samson never gives me any trouble." There was a challenge in her tone.

"Nevertheless," he said, feeling like a teenage boy all over again, suffering through a crush he had no business feeling, "thanks for watching him for me."

Reno came up beside them, divided a look between Wyatt and Remy, then settled his gaze on Wyatt. "Now that you're back, you and me, we need to have a little chat."

"About what?"

"Let's take it outside." He glanced at Remy. "You okay finishing up here?"

She hesitated, looked at him oddly, then nodded slowly. "Of course."

Reno's idea of "taking it outside" was actually moving the discussion to the empty living room. "Don't hurt her, Wyatt."

The warning was so unexpected Wyatt found himself blinking at the other man. "Since when have you become her champion?"

"Remy was there for me when I was at my lowest." His lowest being an addiction to painkillers after his career-ending crash on the slopes.

"And, let me guess," Wyatt said, unable to keep the sneer out of his voice. "You're returning the favor now."

"You could say that." Reno said nothing else on the subject. "She deserves a fresh start with a good man who'll put her first."

Wyatt didn't disagree. Was Reno looking to be that man? "Something going on between you two?"

"Not in the way you mean." Reno's entire countenance turned fierce. "She was one of the first people to realize I was in over my head with the pills. She pushed me to get help and wouldn't let up until I admitted I had a problem. She was there for me through the darkest period of my recovery. No judgment."

"Sounds like Remy."

"I know, right?" Reno rolled his bum shoulder, as if talk of his injury brought back the pain. "She dragged me to physical therapy whenever she could get home. And bullied me through the exercises."

She'd done the same for Wyatt his junior year in high school when he'd suffered an injury that could have kept him out of contention for a scholarship if he'd given in to self-pity.

"I owe her my life," Reno said. "And that's not an exaggeration. I won't see her hurt, not again. Matt did a real number on her and I'm not sure she's fully recovered."

Wyatt's stomach hit his toes. "You think she's still in love with the guy?"

Reno opened his mouth, started to speak, then shut it again. "It's more complicated than that."

"Care to explain?"

"Not my place." Reno rolled his shoulder again, then said, "Anyway, be careful with her, okay, dude?"

Wyatt would do everything in his power to keep from hurting Remy. "Yeah. Okay."

"Good enough." A beat later, Reno was gone.

Wyatt sought out the woman herself. He found the engaged couple instead. He took Hope's hand. "Walker is a lucky man. I wish you many years of happiness together."

"What a sweet thing to say. Thank you, Wyatt. Oh, now look at me. I promised myself I wouldn't cry today." Laughing softly, she swiped at her cheeks. "I've done nothing but all evening."

Wyatt winced. "I didn't mean to upset you."

"These are happy tears." She yanked him into a quick hug. "Thanks for being such a good friend to Walker and... There I go again with waterworks. Phew, I really am emotional."

"Understandable." He shook hands with Walker. "Congratulations. You got a good one."

"Don't I know it." Walker's smile came quick and easy. "Will we see you again tomorrow after church?"

Something warm moved through Wyatt. The Evans family, along with close friends and various stragglers, gathered at this same house every Sunday afternoon as soon as church let out. It was a tradition he'd taken for granted as a kid, but really appreciated now that Samson was in his care. "Wouldn't miss it."

He said good-night and went in search of his nephew. He found Samson in an animated conversation with Remy.

They looked easy with one another, comfortable. Remy was as natural with Samson as if he were her own son. Wyatt swallowed around the knot in his throat. Reno's warning came back to him. *Don't hurt her.*

Wyatt would never hurt Remy, intentionally. His greatest desire was to keep her safe, to cherish her, to erase all her hurts, including the ones he himself had caused. It would not be an easy task. But maybe not as impossible as he once thought. Casey seemed to be on board. What about her other three brothers? Family was everything to Remy. If they disapproved, would she go against their wishes?

Wyatt would never ask her to choose. So, where did that leave him? With a lot to think about.

He predicted another sleepless night.

Chapter Twelve

The next morning, Remy received a frantic phone call from Mrs. Tumi. Meeko Mouse hated his new food and had gone on a hunger strike. The woman was beside herself with worry. After ensuring the cat was drinking water, Remy supplied her former teacher with several suggestions on how to lure the animal to his bowl. She then urged patience and ended the call with one final instruction. "If he continues refusing to eat, bring him by the clinic tomorrow morning."

Mrs. Tumi thanked her. Remy left for church ten minutes behind schedule. She walked into the sanctuary in time to sing the final worship song. She sidled up next to Brent at the back pew and joined in the singing. She couldn't carry a tune, as her brother was happy to remind her every chance he got. That didn't keep her from belting out the words with enthusiasm. She was pretty sure God didn't care what her voice sounded like.

The song ended and everyone took their seats while the associate pastor ran through the weekly announcements. A hand touched Remy's shoulder. She looked up and smiled at Wyatt standing over her. Apparently, she wasn't the only one running late this morning. "Where's Samson?" she asked as she scooted over to make room for him.

Wyatt nodded at Brent, then said, "He wanted to go to Sunday school."

"No kidding? Seriously?"

He nodded again.

This was a huge breakthrough for the boy. Samson hadn't attended Sunday school since his mother went to prison. "That's great."

"It really is." A moment of solidarity passed between them. They continued staring while the lead pastor took the pulpit.

Brandon Stillwell had run in the same crowd as Wyatt and Brent. He'd been the wild one of their group, completely undisciplined, a little scary and a total risk taker, which was saying something since Reno had also been part of their four-man crew.

The rowdy boys had grown up and become good, solid men of integrity, although none had taken the easy path. Brent had needed five years in Africa with Doctors Without Borders to settle him down. Reno had to hit rock bottom before turning the end of his career into a successful business. Wyatt had been the tamest of the four, and the nicest to her. But maybe Remy was just prejudiced since he'd also been front and center of her teenage dreams.

Brandon led the congregation in the opening prayer, then launched into his sermon. He started with a personal story from his high school days that had everyone laughing and nodding and, when he hit the punch line, leaning in. He paused, let the laughter die down, then said, "What I did was stupid and could have ended far worse. Drag racing riding lawn mowers wasn't the smartest way to impress a girl."

More laughter.

"God doesn't keep a tally of our mistakes. He doesn't weigh our good deeds against bad." Brandon would know. He wasn't supposed to amount to anything, that's what the town gossips said, what *everyone* said. The year he spent in jail was hard evidence to support their claim.

Yet, here he was, standing at the pulpit, giving a riveting sermon. "God extends complete forgiveness. He doesn't give any conditions. No loopholes. No condemnation."

Brandon's relaxed demeanor put the congregation at ease. It helped that he was young and good-looking. Lean, athletically built, with piercing silver eyes and spiky hair, Brandon resembled Reno in a lot of ways. And was nothing like him in others.

"Forgiveness starts with surrender…"

Remy turned to look at Brent, unsurprised to catch him slipping out of the pew. It had been six years since his fiancée died in a tragic rock-climbing accident. Although there'd been an inquiry, and the rope manufacturer had been to blame, Brent still held himself responsible for her death. One day, he'd forgive himself. Remy prayed that day came soon.

Wyatt shifted in the pew. His eyes held a thoughtful expression as he listened to Brandon's words. Was he thinking about his sister? Himself? Remy was still considering when Brandon ended his sermon. "I urge we seek forgiveness from those we've wronged and to give forgiveness to those who have hurt us."

The worship band took the stage and launched into the closing song. Brandon said a final prayer and then dismissed the congregation with a reminder that the deadline to sign up for the youth group's petting zoo excursion was this Friday. He smiled at Remy. She smiled back. Wyatt cleared his throat. "You've already scheduled field trips for your petting zoo?"

"Yeah, Brandon hooked me up with the youth pastor who was looking for an animal-themed activity during vacation Bible school."

Wyatt frowned. "You only just got your permit this week."

"I like to plan ahead."

"And if you hadn't gotten the permit?"

"I wasn't worried." She winked at him. "I have connections at the sheriff's office."

He leaned into her, forcing her to stare into his eyes. "You sure about that?"

"Pretty much."

His mouth quirked as he sat back. "I'm not sure whether your initiative is impressive or reckless."

"Neither. It's organized and efficient."

"Uh-huh."

They waited until the aisle was clear to stand. Wyatt stepped out of the pew first, then motioned for Remy to go ahead of him. The atrium was crowded, which was somewhat surprising. Attendance tended to drop during the summer months.

"Will I see you and Samson at Quinn's?" she asked.

Wyatt nodded. "He's looking forward to Sunday dinner with your family."

"What about you? Are you looking forward to time with my family?"

A faint smile touched his lips. "As long as you're there, yes."

His words shouldn't make her head spin. "I'm glad."

Something quite lovely passed between them, an unspoken message that sent her pulse racing.

"Samson will be wondering where I am."

"You should rescue him."

"I should."

He didn't move. Remy didn't move. The moment lasted a few seconds. "Wyatt, I—"

"Remy, I—"

They both broke off, laughed, grinned.

"Go on," he said. "You were about to say something."

Was she? She searched her mind and came away empty. "I—"

She broke off again as she became aware of the man staring at her from just behind Wyatt's left shoulder. Remy blinked hard, fearing that tears would spring to her eyes if she didn't. This couldn't be real. Matt lived in Denver now. He hated coming home to Thunder Ridge. She blinked again. Not a dream. She tried to take a breath, and managed only a choked wheeze.

"Remy?" Wyatt reached out to her. "What is it? What's wrong? You've gone pale."

"I… It's really hot in here." She swallowed. "Too many people." Not people. One person.

"Are you claustrophobic?"

"Really hate crowds," she said through clenched teeth.

Wyatt took her arm. "Let's get you outside."

"No." They would have to pass Matt to get to the exit. "Just give me a minute. I'm fine. Really. Fine."

But she wasn't fine. Matt was still staring at her with indecision in his eyes, as if he was thinking about approaching her but not really sure he should. She had to get away before he decided what to do. The crowd parted and her breath caught in her throat. Matt wasn't alone. His wife of five and a half months stood by his side. Kylie looked happy. She actually *glowed*.

No, Remy thought, praying she was wrong. *Please, God. Not that. Anything but that.*

Needing to know for sure, Remy dropped her gaze to Kylie's midsection. Her no longer impossibly tiny midsection. Remy's gaze shot to Matt. Guilty. Unapologetic, but guilty. As if blinders had been removed from her eyes, Remy saw the past with painful clarity. *We don't suit anymore, Remy. I have political aspirations. I need a wife who can help me attain my goal.*

"I'm taking you outside." Wyatt's voice came at her as if he were speaking through a wall of water.

She shook her head. "I…"

"No argument." Tossing an arm around her shoulders, he tugged her against him. She leaned into his support. And let Wyatt take charge. He led her through the atrium, past Matt and Kylie, straight out the door.

She took her first full breath on the church steps. Out of the corner of her eye, she saw that Matt had followed her out, Kylie dutifully trotting along by his side.

Wyatt could feel Remy's tension melt into him with each breath she took. He'd never seen her this distraught. She didn't strike him as someone who hated closed-in spaces, but now that he thought about it, her desire for a ranch on the edge of the town should have given him a clue.

She was shaking. They were moving toward the steps leading to the parking lot when a masculine voice called out. Remy froze. Then looked at Wyatt in dazed misery.

"Remy?" came the voice again, less tentative, more insistent. "Is that you?"

Slowly, she lifted her chin and turned to face the speaker. "Hello, Matt."

Matt. Although almost the same age, Wyatt had never met Remy's ex-fiancé. The guy had attended boarding schools all his life. Wyatt didn't need to know the man personally to know he was a fool. He'd let Remy go.

"Remy, I thought it was you." The smile the man dropped on her was false and full of perfectly aligned white teeth. Wyatt rarely tamped into his violent side. He had a powerful urge to do so now.

"Matt." Remy's voice sounded strained. "This is Wyatt Holcomb. He's the sheri—"

"I know who you are." Matt shot out his hand. Wyatt shook it automatically. "My father speaks very highly of you."

"Your father is a good man," Wyatt said, unable to keep the note of fury out of his voice. "A solid member of the community."

"He loves his little town." The condescension in the man's tone had Wyatt leveling a cold stare.

"Matt." The woman beside him threw him an impatient glare. "Aren't you going to introduce me to your friends?"

It was then that Wyatt noticed Remy's ex-fiancé wasn't alone. He shifted his attention to the woman. She was near Remy's age, dressed immaculately, and very pretty in a plastic sort of way. She wore her long blond hair pulled back in a severe style that showed off her high cheekbones. She was also pregnant.

"Kylie, this is Sheriff Holcomb," Matt said. "You already know Remy." He smiled with that horrible, toothy slash of teeth.

Remy did not smile back. She did not move.

"When's the baby due?" Wyatt asked, ugly suspicion filling him.

"October 7," Kylie said with remarkable specificity. "I'm twenty-one weeks along. We're in town for the gender reveal with Matt's parents."

Good-old Matt hadn't wasted much time replacing Remy and getting busy building a family. There were a million things he could say to the man, none of them polite.

Since they were standing on the threshold of a house

of God, and Remy needed him to stay calm, Wyatt settled on a benign, "Congratulations."

"Thank you," the pair said in unison, their smiles a little too superior.

Remy swayed slightly. Wyatt pulled her against him. Her thunderstruck expression rolled up to meet his.

He wanted to wrap her in his arms and hold her until that shattered expression on her face went away. The best he could do was remove her from the situation. "Ready to head out?"

She nodded.

"We need to get going ourselves," Matt said, adding to no one in particular, "My mother doesn't like it when I'm late for Sunday dinner. Good seeing you, Remy."

"You, too." Remy said nothing more until Matt and Kylie were well out of sight. "I…" She swallowed. "I have to go."

She started down the steps.

"Remy, wait."

She paused midflight. Just out of Wyatt's reach. Now wasn't the time for words of comfort, not with so many onlookers. He closed the distance and touched her shoulder. "Come with me to get Samson and the three of us will drive over to your sister's house together."

"Can't leave my car. I have to stop at the clinic first anyway." Her voice came out flat, emotionless, and she still hadn't turned around to face him, so Wyatt had no idea what was going on in her head. "Sick patient," she added in a barely there whisper. "Needs me."

Wyatt didn't know if that was true or not, but he let it go. "I'll meet you at Quinn's, then?"

"Okay." Her voice lacked conviction, making him wonder if she would change her mind and avoid her family altogether.

He put the odds at fifty-fifty.

"See you later, Wyatt."

"Yes, you will." This time, he let her retreat. And regretted it immediately.

For several seconds, he debated whether to go after her. And do what? There were too many people in the parking lot. Everything Wyatt wanted to say was for Remy's ears only. He would find the right opportunity to pull her aside at her sister's house. If she didn't show?

He would find her. No matter what, they were going to talk today. This time, he didn't bother calculating the odds.

He was 100 percent certain.

Chapter Thirteen

Remy had no memory of walking through the parking lot. Yet, here she stood next to her SUV, keys in hand, the rasp of her own breathing filling her ears. Had she stopped to speak with friends, smiled at acquaintances? Or had she marched along with her head down? Difficult to say. No matter how hard she examined the contents of her brain, Remy couldn't bring up a single image from the last five minutes. Well, aside from the smug look on Matt's face.

Her heart felt heavy and bruised. She wanted to be alone. Conversely, she couldn't bear the idea of her own company. Swathed in indecision, she debated the wisdom of following through with her promise to Wyatt. He wasn't the problem, not really. It was her family.

They reminded her of all the things she didn't have. Quinn with her loving husband and two gorgeous daughters. Brent with his adorable twins. And then there was Walker and Hope, radiating so much happiness it hurt to look at them.

Remy sighed. She was feeling sorry for herself again. She hated feeling sorry for herself. Because that meant Matt had won. Matt didn't deserve to win. Neither did

Kylie, who'd swooped in the moment Remy was out of the picture.

She had to get out of here.

Fumbling with the car door, she yanked it open on the third try, then sank heavily onto the driver's seat. Hands on the steering wheel, she stared straight ahead, seeing nothing except the image of Matt smiling down at Kylie. All that happiness and smug satisfaction. Remy felt overwhelmed with her own sense of failure.

She didn't want Matt. She'd gotten over him easily enough, maybe too easy. She had walked away with her heart surprisingly intact. Her pride, however, had taken a fatal blow.

As she sat with her hands clutching the steering wheel, she tried to examine her pain objectively. Couldn't do it. Nor could she spend the afternoon with family and friends pretending her life was as wonderful as it looked on the outside. Even if she pulled off the charade, Wyatt knew enough of the truth to ask the questions she wasn't ready to answer.

Decision made, Remy put her car in gear and drove away from the church. She meant to head straight home, to her animals, but she needed to drive for a while. Focusing on the road helped her clear her mind. She meandered through town for an hour, maybe a bit longer. By the time she pulled onto her property, her heart felt lighter. She had a lot to be thankful for: a rewarding career, a home of her own, family and friends that cared about her. Plans already in motion for expansion.

Grasshopper Grange was going to be a success, Remy would make sure of it. She would get her loan, purchase the neighboring property and turn Wildlife World into a premier educational facility for the region. Children would be in her future, just not in the way she'd hoped. Her life could be so much worse.

Attitude adjusted, Remy exited her SUV and nearly dropped the keys on the ground when she caught a flash of brown, woolly fur sashaying in her direction. The alpaca ambled along, her eyelashes fluttering, clearly happy to be alive on this bright, sunny afternoon. On the *wrong* side of her pen.

"Prissy." Remy met the animal at the edge of the driveway. "You naughty, naughty girl. What am I going to do with you?"

The corners of the animal's mouth curled in her perpetual alpaca grin, as if to say *welcome home*. It was too much. Remy's composure broke. "Oh, Prissy."

She buried her face in the alpaca's neck and burst into tears.

Wyatt sat on the front porch of Quinn's house, waiting for Remy to arrive. He gave her half an hour to check on her bogus patient, at which point he texted her. No response. When another fifteen minutes passed, and Remy still hadn't shown, he knew she wasn't coming.

He needed to know why.

He left Samson in Quinn's capable hands and went on the hunt. He found Remy on the edge of her driveway, clutching Prissy for dear life. The muffled sobs were like a knife to his heart. It took tremendous concentration not to drag her into his arms and tell her everything would be all right. He wasn't sure that was true. He'd never seen Remy this upset and vulnerable, not even the day after prom. He hurt for her, her pain as real as if it were his own.

Moving carefully, Wyatt stepped toward her. He waited a beat, then spoke her name softly. A mere whisper on the wind. But she immediately stiffened. "You weren't supposed to come looking for me."

"And yet," he said, "here I am."

Her hands dropped away from Prissy's neck, but she didn't turn around. "There was no need to track me down." Her voice sounded broken. "I'm fine." She wiped furiously at her cheeks. "Seriously, Wyatt, I'm fine."

She was not fine.

"Talk to me, Remy." He placed his hands on her shoulders and gently guided her around to face him. The devastation in her eyes had him asking, "Are you still in love with him?"

Wyatt's gut told him her anguish was bigger than a broken heart. Still, he needed to know.

"I'm not still in love with Matt. I don't know if I was ever in love with him." She pushed out a hard breath. "I think I was more in love with the idea of love."

Wyatt had known this. Deep down he'd known. He wasn't sure how. Except to say that he knew Remy. She wasn't the kind of woman that fell apart over a man. "Then what's got you so upset?"

Before she answered, Prissy shifted between them, reminding Wyatt they had an audience. An audience with a tendency for taking sides, and never his. Right now, the alpaca seemed perfectly calm. But the shirt he wore was one of his favorites. No need to take chances.

He grabbed Prissy's bridle. "Hang tight," he said to Remy. "Be right back."

Avoiding any sudden moves, he escorted the animal to her pen. As if sensing the gravity of the situation, Prissy high-stepped alongside him without a single show of rebellion. "If you behaved like this more often, we could become friends, you know."

The animal made a happy humming sound in her throat.

Wyatt pulled to a stop at the open gate, making a mental note to rethink the latch entirely. Prissy danced in place, eyeing his shirt with a speculative gleam. "Do it," he warned. "And my offer of friendship is off the table."

The alpaca batted her big brown eyes, then dutifully trotted into her pen. "Good girl."

Wyatt returned to where Remy stood watching him, her gaze distant and sad. Although her tears had dried up, he could tell she was hanging on by a thread. The proof was in her rapidly blinking eyes and pale, pale skin. He pulled her into his arms and counted it a victory when she didn't resist.

"Now?" she whispered into his shirt, her voice sounding frail and a little watery. "*Now* you're nice to me?"

"I'm always nice to you."

She wrapped her arms around his waist and pressed her face against his chest. "Oh, Wyatt. Why did you have to come looking for me?"

"You needed me."

Apparently, it was the wrong thing to say. She shoved out of his arms. "I don't need you. I don't need anyone."

"Talk to me, Remy. Tell me why running into your ex-fiancé upset you so much."

She stepped further away from him. "I can't tell you."

"Oh, but you can. And you will. You'll start by explaining—"

Hearing the *cop* in his voice, Wyatt cut off his own words. The last thing Remy needed was an interrogation. He tried a different approach. Taking her hand, he pulled her to the porch steps. He waited for her to sit beside him to say, "I want to help you, Remy. But I need to know what I'm working with first."

She placed her elbows on her thighs, leaned forward and dropped her gaze. "You'll think less of me."

"Never."

"Trust me on this. You won't look at me the same."

"Remy." Wyatt slung an arm over her shoulders, then retreated when she flinched. "Remy," he said again. "There is nothing you can say that will change how I feel about you. Nothing."

"Okay. I'll say it quick." She hesitated. Then words started tumbling out of her mouth, coming right on top of one another. "It started with a routine checkup. I'm young, healthy, nothing to worry about, right? Except, maybe not so healthy, after all. I'd been having some issues. Nothing that concerned me, not really, but I brought it up with my doctor. She had some ideas as to what was causing my pain."

"What kind of pain?"

"Not important." Lifting her chin, Remy went on to explain about a series of tests her doctor ordered. "She was reluctant to give a definitive diagnosis, but the results all pointed to the same thing."

Wyatt's heart dropped to his toes. "Cancer?"

"No." She shut her eyes, sighed, opened them again. "Endometriosis. Lots of women suffer from the condition. It's painful, but not life-threatening."

Wyatt wasn't seeing the problem, and then he did when she said, "Bottom line, the odds are stacked against me of ever conceiving a child."

Wyatt heard the devastation in her voice. Her misery was a living, breathing thing vibrating between them. He understood her pain and grieved with her. Remy adored children. "I'm sorry."

She didn't respond. He wasn't sure she even heard him. Her gaze remained focused on a spot off in the distance. "I'm sorry," he said again.

"When I told Matt, he said all the right things. He

claimed my diagnosis was no big deal. If I couldn't have children the old-fashioned way, no problem, we'd try other methods. If all else failed, we would adopt. And that was that." She heaved another, longer sigh. "Or so I thought."

Although several responses came to mind, Wyatt stayed silent, letting Remy tell her story.

"Matt broke off our engagement two weeks after my diagnosis."

From that one sentence, Wyatt understood everything.

"When he broke up with me, he told me—" She stopped, shook her head, tried again. "He told me I didn't fit in with his plans for the future. He has political aspirations, after all, and I wasn't suited to be a politician's wife."

"He actually said those words?"

She nodded. "I asked if he was breaking off our engagement because I couldn't have children. He said that wasn't the reason."

"And you believed him?"

"I had my doubts," she admitted. "His answer was too pat. But today? When I saw that Kylie was pregnant? It… caught me off guard."

Wyatt hadn't liked the man on sight. Now he really disliked him. "Matt's a fool."

Remy gave him a watery smile. "You have to say that, you're my friend."

"This isn't a hard one to figure out, Remy. He's a fool. He let you go." What man in his right mind would walk away from this amazing woman? *You did.*

Suddenly, Wyatt saw all the lost years with alarming clarity. Sure, he'd been a teenager. Nothing but an idealistic kid with big dreams. But Remy's brothers had been wrong about one thing. Wyatt hadn't been toying with her affections. His interest in her had been sincere.

Could they have built something from their mutual attraction? He would never know. Could they start over and try again? He wanted to find out.

Wyatt was still thinking about Remy later that night after he put Samson to bed. He spent the next two hours on the internet researching endometriosis. Remy was right, mostly. Worst-case scenario she could have considerable trouble conceiving, especially as she aged. But there was nothing definitive to say she couldn't conceive. Matt really was a fool.

The next morning, Wyatt came to the same conclusion. Remy's ex-fiancé had made a huge mistake letting Remy go. She was well rid of the guy.

Wyatt rehearsed in his mind what he would say to her. But when he dropped off Samson at the animal clinic, she seemed back to her old self. He hadn't expected that. "You sleep okay?" he asked.

"I'm good, Wyatt. Thanks." Her voice sounded normal, but she didn't quite meet his gaze. That alone told him she wasn't fully recovered. If he had more time, and they were alone, he would have pressed the issue. As things stood, he left her, promising himself they would revisit the conversation another time.

His morning got hectic after that. The calls through dispatch came in rapid-fire succession. Still a deputy down, Wyatt had to answer two himself. The first was a code violation by a construction company. The second was to break up a fight out at the lake between two teenage boys trading punches over a girl.

Wyatt arrived at his office in a foul mood, brooding over the situation, knowing the boys would surely be back at each other's throats as soon as he left. He could use a shot of coffee. No, actually, what he wanted was Remy.

He was too busy to stop by the animal clinic. A text would have to do. Samson behaving?

She responded with three red hearts, followed by We're playing hooky. We're out at Casey's airstrip cuddling puppies and teaching them tricks.

Wyatt sighed.

Samson and Roscoe say hi.

He sighed again. Remy was definitely feeling better today.

He was called out to Thunder Ridge Rides and Guides next. The all-purpose adventure company provided hiking, biking, skiing, climbing and rafting excursions.

As the highest officer in the county, Wyatt had to use a variety of skill sets in the name of law and order. Over the next several hours, he coordinated with the fire department and a volunteer S&R team in an effort to rescue a young couple who'd left their group despite the guide's warning. They'd encountered a protective mama bear and her cub. The two had taken refuge on a tree branch that collapsed under their weight and sent them over the edge of a cliff.

Thankfully, this occurred after the bears had vacated the vicinity. The husband sustained a broken arm and leg, while the wife had received nothing more than a few scratches.

They were both lucky to be alive.

Once they were rescued off the cliff and were on their way to the hospital, Wyatt returned to his office. He received two more calls that took him out of the building.

He was barely settled in his chair when Doris appeared at his desk, hands on her hips. "You're being run ragged. When are you going to hire that new deputy?"

Wyatt answered in what he considered a heroically neutral tone. "After I interview possible candidates, which can't occur until you send me the file of resumés you promised to pull together."

"You haven't checked your email today."

Wyatt hated it when Doris stated the obvious. "As you yourself pointed out, I've been a little busy today."

"Well, right now you're not busy." She arrowed a finger in his direction. "The file is sitting in your inbox. I took the liberty of organizing the candidates with the most work experience and commendations, to the least. Work your way down from top to bottom."

And that was why Wyatt put up with the woman's snark. "You're amazing."

"Don't I know it." She left his office, but not before she said, "Happy hunting, Sheriff."

"Thanks." Wyatt weeded through the list, then sent Doris a new file with his top five candidates and a request to set up first-round phone interviews ASAP.

He checked his phone, saw that Remy had sent him another text. Heading out to McCoy's now.

What's happening at McCoy's?

He's teaching Samson and me the fine art of face painting.

Why?

Possible petting zoo activity.

Okay, that made sense. Have fun.

Remy responded with a thumbs-up.

Wyatt stared at his phone, briefly wondering what, exactly, was involved with face painting. One sure way to find out. He clicked on the search engine and took a tour of several websites before Doris appeared at his desk again. "We have an intercom system, you know," he reminded her.

She ignored him. "There's an emergency out at the senior center."

Wyatt checked his watch. "My shift ends in twenty minutes. Have Brian take the call."

"You were requested by name. So, you better get over there right away." Expression giving nothing away, she reached across his desk and switched off his computer monitor. "The caller said it's urgent."

"Was someone hurt?"

"Guess you'll find out more once you get there." Doris was surprisingly nonchalant for an urgent call, which indicated this was probably one of those calls. The kind that was urgent only from the caller's point of view. Still, he wasn't taking any chances. Wyatt hustled over to the senior center. Not sure what he was walking into, he texted Remy before entering the building. I may be late picking up Samson. You okay with that?

It'll cost you.

He smiled. Yep, Remy was feeling better. He shot back another text. How much?

We'll work out the details later. She'd added a winky-face emoji.

Smiling, Wyatt returned his phone to its case and entered the senior center. Built by a prospector who'd made his fortune in the silver mines, the building itself had been updated several times in its 120 years of life, the most recent five years ago. Lots of history and charm mingled with modern conveniences that included a small movie theater, a spectacular rec room that doubled as a ballroom for Friday night dances and a one-lane bowling alley in the basement.

Wyatt stepped inside the building, looked around, sighed. All quiet. He approached the welcome desk, where a beefy guy somewhere in his late thirties sat reading a paperback novel by Steinbeck. He wore a handwritten badge that said Leo on the first line and Volunteer on the second.

Leo-the-volunteer greeted Wyatt with a smile full of crooked teeth. "Hey, Sheriff. What are you doing here?"

"My office received a call about an emergency."

"No kidding?" Two bushy eyebrows slammed together. "No one told me anything about an emergency."

Wyatt frowned, then heard, "Sheriff! At last, you're here. We've been waiting for you."

The speaker was none other than Mavis Miller, Reno's grandmother. She was a lively older woman, full of personality and somewhere between eighty and a hundred— even Reno didn't know her real age. She favored bright polyester tracksuits, and was the owner of the Wash and Spins, a hybrid dance studio and laundromat. She currently wore her hair in her signature ballerina bun.

"Mavis?" He'd been calling her by her first name at her insistence since he was twelve. "You call my office about an emergency?"

"I did, indeed." She patted her bun as if to make sure it was still there.

"What's your emergency?"

"We're down a man. I called my grandson, but he was unavailable. You're here now. And…" She ran her gaze from the top of his head to the tips of his boots. "You'll do quite nicely."

"Hold up. What do you mean you're *down a man*?"

"You'll see." She took his arm and led him down a hallway toward the rec room. Not a single hint of urgency rolled off her. Getting a real bad feeling, Wyatt attempted to pull his arm free.

Mavis held on tighter, then steered him into the rec room.

"We have our man," she announced. "Class can now begin."

"Class?" he croaked. "What class?"

"Our Monday night ballroom dance lessons, of course. We're a little heavy on female participants this week." Wyatt looked around and took a quick inventory. There wasn't a single person in the room with a Y chromosome. Not one.

What had he just walked into? "Where's the emergency, Mavis?"

"It's like I told you. We're down a man." Mavis ran her gaze over him again. "You're a man, right?"

"Yes…"

"You can dance, right?"

"Not even a little bit."

"You will when I'm through with you." While Wyatt was adjusting to the horror of that unsettling statement, Mavis dragged him deeper into the room. *Dragged* being the operative word.

He counted eleven occupants, all of whom hadn't seen seventy for at least a decade. A few wore flowing dresses with big, billowy skirts. Most were dressed in variations of tracksuits similar to the one Mavis wore, plus sparkles. Lots of sparkles.

He bent down to stare Mavis straight in the eye. "Let me get this straight. Your emergency is that you need a man, any man, basically a warm body to partner with your—" How did he put this delicately? "—students?"

"Don't sell yourself short, Sheriff. You're much more than just a warm body."

Agreement came in the form of hoots and whistles. "Apparently, I need to explain the definition of *an emergency*."

As if sensing she was about to be on the wrong end of a lecture, Mavis wagged her finger at him. "You are a public servant, Sheriff. You were elected to serve the public. We—" she swept her hand in a wide arc to include her students "—are the public, aren't we?"

She wasn't wrong. And to be fair, this wasn't the first time Wyatt had been called out to an emergency that wasn't actually an emergency. "I'll stay for one dance, Mavis. One."

A woman approached him with a speculative gleam in her eye. Wyatt couldn't recall her name, but she looked vaguely familiar. "You've grown up real nice, Sheriff. I used to change your diapers when you were a baby."

Wyatt decided to be a good sport. "I don't remember that at all."

This received a round of laughter.

"All right, girls, and boy." Mavis winked at him. "Let's get started, shall we?"

Eleven pairs of eyes locked on him. In that moment, he understood how a fox felt right before the hounds were released.

Mavis motioned for Wyatt's previous babysitter to take her place as his partner. "Stand with your feet hip distance apart," she told him. "And hold Genevieve like this." She placed his hands in the proper position, one on the woman's shoulder, the other at her waist. "Now. Step your left foot forward like this. Your right one next. And then the left again."

Public servant, he reminded himself as he followed Mavis's directions. As a former athlete, he understood the basic mechanics of using his mind to control his body. He could still pick a target out of two dozen moving bodies, pull his arm back and hit his man with spectacular accuracy. The waltz, he quickly discovered, was a billion times more complicated.

"The rhythm is *one*, two, three. *One*, two, three. Got it?"

"Sure thing." Wyatt guided his partner around the room, watching his feet and muttering, "*One*, two, three. *One*, two, three."

He'd barely found the rhythm when he was passed off to the next student.

One, two, three. *One*, two, three.

This time, he made an entire circuit of the room before someone yelled, "Are you done with the boy yet?"

The question came from a member of the tracksuit set. The women in the long, sparkly dresses were immensely more polite.

One, two, three.

The music finally, mercifully, stopped. Wyatt all but ran for door.

Mavis blocked his exit. "You're a natural, Sheriff."

"You're just saying that to restore my pride."

"Not at all. You're a very quick study." She patted his arm in a grandmotherly gesture that belied the wily look in her eyes. "Next week we'll attempt the foxtrot."

"Next week?" he choked out. "Nope. I'm busy next week."

Mavis countered his objection with two succinct words. "Public. Servant."

Wyatt groaned.

Chapter Fourteen

Almost as soon as Remy turned onto her property, the clear skies gave way to dark, ominous clouds rolling in off the mountains. "We better conquer our chores before the rain starts," she said to Samson.

"What about Roscoe?"

Remy checked on the puppy currently asleep in the crate she'd buckled onto the back seat. "He's not going anywhere." She lowered the back windows to half-mast. "We'll bring him inside with us once we're finished feeding the animals."

"Do you think Uncle Wyatt will let me keep him?"

Remy knew better than to ask. "We agreed that Roscoe would live on the ranch with me."

"But he's mine, right?"

The boy had posed this same question a dozen times on the ride from Casey's airstrip to McCoy's art studio. He'd brought it up again while McCoy showed Remy how to paint a Spider-Man mask. "Roscoe is definitely your dog. But remember, Samson. As we discussed when we left my brother's house, your uncle is too busy to help you take care of him."

"I remember," Samson said. "Roscoe stays on the ranch for now. Maybe forever if that's what Uncle Wyatt wants."

The boy *had* been listening. "Exactly."

"Okay. I'll get to my chores now." Samson was out the door several seconds ahead of Remy. It was nice no longer having to tell the boy what to do or where to start. She left him with King Henry while she fed the rest of the animals in the outdoor pens.

She reentered the barn to the sound of Samson's solemn voice. "You know, King Henry, you don't have to let the bigger kids ride you."

The pony responded with an impatient snort.

"I could be your only rider. I'm not too big. And I promise not to hurt you."

Smiling, Remy popped her head into the stall and simply watched the little boy smooth his hand down the pony's spine. "Sometimes grown-ups don't listen to me, either. But Miss Remy says if I keep telling them what I need, they'll eventually hear me."

Remy didn't remember saying that.

"Anyway." Samson fell silent a moment, then began chattering again. "You're under my care now. I'll make sure you're safe. Like Uncle Wyatt makes sure I'm safe."

Remy's eyes filled with unshed tears. Samson was such a sweet little boy. It was clear he loved his uncle. She wiped at her eyes. The movement must have given her away. Samson's shoulders stiffened.

"I hope I'm not interrupting," she said conversationally.

Samson stepped away from the pony, his little cheeks turning a bright red. "I wasn't doing anything wrong."

"No, you weren't. You were talking to King Henry like you would a good friend."

"Yeah, so?" He lifted his chin at a defiant angle. "Lots of people talk to animals."

"Yes, they do." Very gently tilting the little boy's face upward, she looked past the face paint, straight into a pair of worried eyes. "But very few understand their replies. That makes you special, Samson. Never forget that." She dropped her hands. "You finished in here?"

He nodded.

"Let's wake up Roscoe and go inside the house." Remy walked Samson through feeding the puppy. Then she filled Farrell's bowl with kitten food high in meat protein. Scooby got his dinner last.

While the animals ate, she and Samson settled at the kitchen table, him with his blueprints. Her with her laptop. "Before you get too involved, I have something for you."

"Gummy bears?" he asked, eyes wide and hopeful.

She laughed. "Not candy, no."

The boy gave her a grin reminiscent of his uncle. "Never hurts to ask."

"Never does. Hang tight. I'll be right back." Two minutes later, she placed the gift on the table next to Samson's backpack.

He eyed the tube with suspicion. "What is it?"

"It's a storage tube like the ones architects use for their blueprints. It's waterproof."

Samson touched the plastic cylinder. "I really like the color."

Remy did, too. The electric blue matched the blue in the boy's Spider-Man face paint. "The end cap is removable. Here, let me show you how it works." She twisted off the lid, pulled it away from the tube, then screwed it back on. "The strap is adjustable. Let's see if it fits."

It didn't.

She made a few adjustments and tried again. "Perfect. Now, let's see if your blueprints fit inside the tube." Taking great care, Remy rolled the ever-growing stack of papers, then slid them inside the tube. "Another perfect fit."

Samson grinned. "I love it. Thanks, Miss Remy."

"You're very welcome. Ready to get to work?"

Her suggestion was met with an approving nod. They were barely ten minutes into their individual projects when her phone dinged with an incoming text from Reno. Take a look at this. You will not regret it. You're welcome.

Remy frowned. That wasn't cryptic at all.

Seriously, take a look. Reno added a few laughing emojis before going silent.

Not sure what to expect, she pressed on the link Reno had provided. The screen immediately filled with an amateur video taken on someone's cell phone.

"What in the world?" Remy squinted at the screen. She felt her heart jolt as she realized the video was of Wyatt dressed in his sheriff's uniform, surrounded by a bunch of little old ladies, including Reno's grandmother Mavis. The crowd separated, and then…

Wyatt was spinning one of the ladies around the room. There was some sort of old-fashioned song playing in the background and…*no*. Was he actually counting out loud? Remy closed her eyes and listened. He was. Wyatt was counting. "*One*, two, three," he said, putting emphasis on the *one*. "*One*, two, three. *One*, two, three."

Wyatt was passed off to another partner. And then another. At one point there was a minor scuffle, before yet another lady claimed her turn. He should have looked ridiculous, waltzing around the room, counting in time with the music, his face scrunched in concentration. He didn't look ridiculous at all. He looked adorable. And sweet, and if she wasn't already fond of the man, she would have been a goner right then and there.

"Samson. Come over here. You gotta see this."

The little boy leaned over the phone. "What is Uncle Wyatt doing?"

"He's waltzing."

"What's waltzing?"

A new voice entered the conversation. "It's a type of dance between two people." Wyatt stepped into the kitchen, Farrell wrapped around his neck. "I knocked. You didn't answer so I let myself in." His eyes narrowed. "Please tell me you're watching a video of puppies frolicking in a field of flowers."

A surge of warmth and happiness and so much affection caused the back of her eyes to sting. "It's much sweeter than puppies."

"Maybe I should be the judge of that." He took the phone and, with a perplexed frown, glared at the screen. "Someone actually took a video of my complete and utter humiliation?"

"It's not humiliating, Wyatt. It's sweet."

His expression darkened. Handing Remy the phone, he reached up and rubbed the space between his eyebrows. "Can't a man have any secrets in this town?"

"Not if he's a sheriff with a heart of gold." She set the phone on the table and without thinking too hard about what she was doing, lifted onto her toes and kissed his cheek.

Samson made a gagging sound. "Gross. You kissed my uncle."

"On the cheek," she clarified, gaze hooked with Wyatt's.

"Why did you do that?" Both man and boy asked the question in unison and with identical expressions of masculine bafflement.

Smiling now, Remy divided a look between the two. "The kiss was a thank-you for being so nice to the ladies at the senior center."

Again, man and boy spoke at the same time. "Oh."

"Seriously, Wyatt, that was a really sweet thing to do."

"Don't be too impressed. I was tricked into cooperating. It started with a call to dispatch and went downhill from there." By the time he explained the entire story, Remy was laughing.

Samson, too.

Wyatt still didn't seem to see the humor in the situation. He would, Remy decided, once the humiliation wore off. "What I don't understand is how you found a video of the whole sordid affair so quickly. I left the senior center less than thirty minutes ago."

"Reno sent me a link."

"Reno. Of course. What a guy." Wyatt shook his head. He seemed to think for a long moment before adding, "Now that I think about it, I'm pretty sure he was behind this disaster."

"The video or the dance class?"

"Both."

He glanced around the room, did a double take at the animal currently climbing on top of Scooby's head. "Remy, don't know how to tell you this, but your dog has sprouted a puppy from his ear."

"That's Roscoe," Samson said, rushing to pick up the animal. "He's mine. But he has to live here on the ranch because you're too busy for a puppy right now."

"I can explain," Remy said, but Wyatt was already shaking his head.

"I think I get the picture."

Then why wasn't he reading her her rights? As if he could hear her thoughts, he opened his mouth to speak, then closed it and spun to address Samson instead. "What is that on your face? No, don't tell me. It's McCoy's handiwork."

"Actually, it's mine," Remy said. "McCoy walked me through the steps. But I did the actual painting."

Wyatt studied Samson's face with an unreadable expression. Then, he smiled and said, "Not bad. Not bad at all."

Remy basked in the compliment, for three full seconds.

"Wait a minute. Just hold up." She gave Wyatt a quick once-over much like the one Mavis had given him on the video. "Who are you and what have you done with my friend Wyatt?"

"Oh, I'm the same man." He unwrapped Farrell from around his neck and passed the ferret into her waiting arms. "I'm just seeing the world in a whole new light these days."

Remy wasn't buying it. Something had changed. As soon as the thought came to her, she had her answer. Wyatt wasn't seeing the world in a whole new light. He was seeing *her* in a whole new light.

Pain rocketed from her head to the pit of her stomach. She had to cover her mouth to keep from sobbing. *Oh, Wyatt, not you, too.* Remy had warned him this would happen. She'd known he would think less of her once he knew her secret.

Regret moved through her. Bone-deep sorrow came next. She'd not been expecting this. She'd honestly thought she and Wyatt had something special. But he was no different from any other man she'd told about her endometriosis. First Matt with his rejection. Then Reno with his pity. And now Wyatt with his seeing the world in a *whole new light*.

"Remy? What's wrong?"

She looked down at the ferret in her arms, feeling weird and light-headed. Her vision was tinged a light gray, as though her eyes couldn't quite focus. "Nothing's wrong," she lied, clutching Farrell closer. "Samson, why don't you show your uncle your new blueprint holder."

She was disproportionately relieved the boy took his cue and that Wyatt let the moment pass. She held it together until they left. Only then, when she was completely alone with her beloved animals, did she sink to the ground and let the tears come.

Wyatt stood in Samson's bathroom, contemplating the Spider-Man mask with genuine puzzlement. He couldn't deny Remy had wielded her paintbrush with remarkable skill. He was impressed every time he got a good look at Samson's face. He'd been prepared to send her a text reiterating how much he admired her artwork. But then he'd discovered the paint didn't come off with soap and water. Adding drama to the already tense situation, Samson decided he hated getting his face wet. News to Wyatt. The boy never had a problem before.

Time to call in the big guns. Wyatt dug out his phone and scrolled through his list of contacts. Deciding to go to the source, he called McCoy. The other man's response was quick and to the point. "Apply cold cream."

"I have no idea what that is."

McCoy explained, sort of. The man's words only confused Wyatt further. "Where am I supposed to get a jar of that at this hour?"

"Try a drugstore."

Easier said than done. It was after nine and Walgreens didn't deliver. Short of wrapping Samson up and driving back into town, Wyatt was stuck until morning.

McCoy told him that the paint was nontoxic. A few more hours wouldn't do any harm. "Have a good night, Wyatt."

Wyatt was pretty sure he heard laughter in McCoy's voice. He pocketed the phone and shook his head. Artists, he thought, were a strange bunch.

Refusing to give up, he turned the water back on in the sink, tested the temperature, then wet the washcloth again. Samson darted for the door. Wyatt blocked his exit. After another round of "you're not leaving this bathroom," and Samson's pleas to "let me go," Wyatt applied the washcloth to the boy's face.

Shaking his head back and forth, Samson picked a new battle to wage. And at exactly the wrong time. "I want Roscoe to live with us."

"He's fine living at Remy's."

"I want Roscoe to live with us. Did you hear me, Uncle Wyatt?"

"I heard you." He was pretty sure the neighbors in a four-block radius heard the boy.

"We aren't having this discussion right now."

"I. Want. Roscoe."

Wyatt remained firm and continued working on the face paint. With zero success. The tears came next. And then, the gut punch. "You're hurting me."

He let the boy go. He'd buy the cold cream in the morning. Or maybe throw himself on Remy's mercy and beg her to remove what she so brilliantly applied in the first place.

The next morning presented Wyatt with another series of complications. Samson was up an hour before his usual time. Wyatt heard the boy stirring and prayed he'd fall back to sleep. Wyatt was attempting to fit in another half hour himself when Samson ran into his bedroom wearing his Spider-Man T-shirt and a pair of filthy blue jeans. Both had been relegated to the dirty clothes hamper for good reason.

"Uncle Wyatt, Uncle Wyatt, Uncle Wyatt! Is now a good time to talk about Roscoe?"

"Not until after I've had my coffee." He hauled himself out of bed. "Go play with your Legos while I shower."

"Okay." Samson bounced out of the room.

Wyatt showered and managed a quick shave before feeding Samson a breakfast of cereal and buttered toast. A staple these days and certainly more nutritious than the gooey cinnamon rolls his mother used to serve the boy. Although he consumed the food entirely too fast, Samson ate every bite without a single argument.

Lulled into a sense of confidence, Wyatt hustled him upstairs for a quick change followed by teeth brushing and hair combing. That's when things fell apart. Samson refused to wear anything but the T-shirt he had on now, arguing, "It matches my face."

"It won't once we wash off the paint."

"But I don't want to wash off the paint."

"But you can't spend the rest of your life wearing a Spider-Man mask," Wyatt informed him.

"Why not?"

Wyatt knew better than to list the many reasons, especially the ones that supported proper hygiene. He'd learned a few things in the months since becoming the boy's guardian. "How about you wear the mask today and then we'll decide next steps tonight?"

It was a terrible idea. He was setting himself up for this exact same argument in twelve hours. Samson was not one to let something go once he got it into his head, a trait he'd inherited straight from his mother. Chip off the old block. Wyatt tried not to sigh.

The next hitch in their regular schedule came after Samson brushed his teeth. This time, the boy expressed his unhappiness with Wyatt's parenting skills during the wetting and brushing of his hair. He howled—actually howled—every time the hairbrush caught in a knot, which happened to be often. Wyatt tried to be gentle, but the boy was a restless sleeper. Tangles were a foregone conclusion from the constant tossing and turning. Short of buzz-cutting the hair, they would both have to endure the torture.

At last, he had Samson loaded in his truck. It wasn't until Wyatt was halfway between his house and Remy's animal clinic that he realized he'd left the boy's lunch on the kitchen counter. Right next to his wallet.

He didn't have time to go back for either. At the next stoplight, he texted a desperate SOS to Remy. Her response came immediately. No worries. He can share mine.

Relieved, Wyatt texted back. You're a lifesaver. I owe you one.

Her response made him laugh. Your account is filling up quickly, Sheriff.

We'll discuss payment later.

Maybe he'd take her out to dinner. Just the two of them. He'd show her just how nice he could be when he set his mind to it. Samson and his mother weren't the only ones who'd inherited the stubborn gene. The idea of taking Remy on a date had Wyatt smiling.

He was still smiling when he rolled into his office a half hour later. Remy had been her usual friendly self during the Samson exchange, if a bit distant. She'd promised to remove the face paint, much to Wyatt's appreciation. Still, he wondered if she was still upset over her encounter with her former fiancé. They hadn't really spoken since she'd told him her story. No moment had presented itself. Wyatt definitely needed significant time alone with Remy.

He would make it happen as soon as he found a reliable babysitter for Samson. Then, Wyatt would be very nice to Remy. He'd give her his best. Better than his best.

What could possibly go wrong?

Chapter Fifteen

A lot could go wrong, Wyatt learned several days later. He was no closer to setting up a date with Remy than when he'd come up with the idea. Not from want of trying. He'd asked her out, twice, making sure to keep the suggestion casual and low-key. "What do you say we go out to dinner sometime?"

She'd responded with basically the same four words. "Okay, sure. Why not," she'd answered without actually looking at him. And probably not really hearing him. He'd left it at that the first time. He'd pressed harder the second. "When's a good time for you?"

"I don't know. Maybe after Grasshopper Grange's grand opening."

Since the petting zoo's grand opening was two days away, Wyatt decided to back off. He could be a patient man. Remy wasn't going anywhere. She was home for good. That alone was worth celebrating. Maybe he'd lead with that when he asked her out again.

In the meantime, Wyatt took his favorite nephew out to dinner at the Latte Da. Mrs. Brooks herself sat them at their usual table in the back corner of the restaurant. The seat gave Wyatt a full view of the diner, a must for a sea-soned lawman.

He and Samson placed their orders with their favorite waitress, Noreen. Cheeseburgers and fries for them both. Samson laid out his most recent rendering of his dream day care and got to work. Wyatt watched, awe filling him. The little boy had a real gift and an eye for detail. The bell over the door jangled. And in walked Remy.

She'd changed into jeans, an oversize shirt and com-bat boots. She looked both feminine and tough, and Wy-att's stomach knotted with familiar tension. He should be used to the sensation by now. Practically immune. On the contrary, he doubted he'd ever get used to his visceral re-action to Remy.

The woman blazed through life with relentless energy. She kept him guessing, and he liked it. He liked her. Wyatt really needed to set up that date. He had things to say to Remy. He was through playing by rules set in the distant past. Time to blaze a new trail.

"Miss Remy, Miss Remy. Over here!" Samson waved wildly, attempting to get her attention. And succeeding, along with everyone else's in the diner. "Come sit with us."

She lifted her chin in acknowledgment, but took her sweet time making her way through the diner. She stopped to talk to people she knew, pausing to look at a child's col-oring, a favorite toy, a loose tooth. At last, she stopped at their table.

"Hi, Samson." Turning her head, she added, "Hello, Wyatt."

"Remy."

After that intellectually stimulating conversation, she sat in the chair directly opposite his and proceeded to ig-nore him completely. Even with her face firmly turned to-ward Samson, Wyatt could feel her tension. She seemed uncomfortable around him. That gave him pause. Had he done something to upset her?

"What are you working on?" Remy asked Samson.

The boy turned the paper so she could see. She studied the drawing.

Wyatt studied her.

Only a small portion of his brain functioned like a normal human being. The rest went into cop mode, gathering details: the whiff of pine and outdoors, the contrast of coal-black hair against creamy white skin, the intense blue of her eyes. The stark lighting also revealed the dark circles under those amazing eyes. There were also lines of fatigue on her face. She wasn't sleeping well. Wyatt knew the signs. He'd seen them in his mirror just this morning. He knew why he wasn't sleeping.

He wasn't sure what was keeping Remy up at night. Probably not wise to ask her in front of Samson. He retrieved his phone, typed out a quick text and pressed Send. Remy's phone dinged an instant later. Setting down the paper, she dug out the device and read his four-word text. We need to talk.

She lifted her head, a silent question in her eyes.

"Not now," he said. "I'll call you later tonight."

She nodded, looking confused and wary. He felt the same. A phone call wasn't their usual mode of communication, and definitely not as good as face-to-face. However, Wyatt didn't want to wait for a better time. So much for being a patient man.

"What do you think about the addition?" Samson's question gave her a little jolt.

Recovering quickly, Remy glanced back at the drawing. "What am I looking at, exactly?"

"Right there." The boy pointed to a spot on the page.

"It's a special doggie day care for kids to bring their puppies with them."

"Clever. I like it."

"Me, too." Samson slid Wyatt a sidelong glance, then grinned at Remy. "Wouldn't it be great to have your puppy around all day long?"

"Really great." The two shared a smile that was full of meaning, as if they were plotting a way to take over the world one puppy at a time. Or rather take over Wyatt's life one puppy at a time. A puppy named Roscoe. Not happening.

"Are you joining us for dinner?" he asked Remy.

"I'm meeting Brent and the girls. They should be here any minute."

Samson scowled. "I like Harper okay, but Kennedy is bossy."

"Samson." Wyatt said his nephew's name with a stern note in his voice. "We've discussed this."

"But, Uncle Wyatt, she *is* bossy."

The boy was missing the point. "Nevertheless, how do we speak about girls?"

Samson heaved a weighty sigh. "I'm not supposed to say bad things about them, not even if they're super bossy and don't understand anything about anything and aren't likeable *at all*."

Wyatt heaved his own weighty sigh. So much to unpack in his nephew's response. Wyatt kept it simple. "Not even then. Got it?"

Another sigh. "Yeah."

"Yes."

"Yes."

Remy looked away, but not before Wyatt caught her trying to hide a smile. Glad someone found this amusing. The bell jingled over the door and Samson's face fell. "They're here."

The twins saw their aunt and rushed over. Remy wrapped her nieces in a group hug, turning herself into a human sandwich between two giggling little girls.

Brent came over soon after. He nodded to Wyatt, then grinned down at Samson. "Hey, kiddo. What's that you're working on?"

Samson puffed up with little-boy pride under the adult attention. "I'm redesigning my old day care. The building has serious structural problems."

"Does it now?" Brent asked.

Wyatt shrugged. "News to me."

"Not that I care, or anything. I don't go there anymore." Samson lowered his gaze and hunched over the drawing, making Wyatt think the boy cared very much. "But it's okay because I get to spend every day with Miss Remy and her animals."

Brent patted the boy's shoulder. "Not a bad deal."

"We miss you," the twins said simultaneously.

He didn't respond.

Kennedy wedged herself between her father and Samson, her little face scrunched into a serious expression. "How come you don't come to day care anymore?"

Looking at her oddly, Samson started to say something, then quickly looked away and shrugged. "I just don't, okay?"

Kennedy's bottom lip started to tremble. "Is it because of me? Am I the reason you don't go there anymore?"

Samson shrugged again. "I don't know."

"It is, isn't it?" Her eyes started to fill with tears. "You can't come to day care anymore because of me."

"You don't have to cry, Kennedy." Looking uncomfortable and slightly tortured, Samson shifted around in his chair. "It was my own fault. I shouldn't have put critters in your cubby. It was mean."

Wyatt blinked, literally stunned speechless by his nephew's acceptance of the blame. A remarkable transformation from the boy he'd marched out of the day care weeks ago. Wyatt cleared his throat, but the surge of emotions couldn't be swallowed back. Pride. Relief. A spattering of hope he wasn't failing completely.

"Well, I thought it was funny," Harper announced from her spot next to Remy. "You did, too. Didn't you, Daddy?"

Before Brent could respond, Kennedy tapped Samson on the shoulder. "It was kind of funny," she admitted in a stage whisper. "Once Daddy knew I was okay, he laughed." She swung her gaze up to her father. "Didn't you, Daddy?"

"I may have laughed," Brent admitted, winking at Samson.

"Really?" Samson asked, wide-eyed and hopeful.

"You got style, kid."

Samson beamed.

"Soooo… Can we be friends, now?" Kennedy asked.

Horror filled Samson's eyes. "Boys can't be friends with girls."

"Yes, they can. My sister and I talked about it. Isn't that right, Harper? We're friends with Samson," she said. "Aren't we?"

"The very best of friends," Harper chimed in.

Samson blinked at Kennedy. "I…" He fell silent.

The little girl just kept smiling, saying nothing, giving him a chance to think over her offer. Samson held out for three full seconds, then caved like a sinkhole in quicksand. "I guess we can be friends."

The conversation turned to whether hot dogs were better than hamburgers. Wyatt flashed back to his own childhood. A long-forgotten memory materialized, seemingly out of nowhere, as if it had been imbedded in his brain waiting for this exact moment to present itself. He hadn't been much older than Samson when Remy had made a similar declaration about friendship. Wyatt had told her that boys couldn't be friends with girls. Remy had smiled at him, just like Kennedy was smiling at Samson. And just like his nephew, Wyatt had instantly caved. *I guess we can be friends.*

Noreen arrived with their meals at that moment.

"Well, now that we're all friends, come on, girls. You, too, Brent." Remy rose from her chair. "Let's leave the boys to their burgers."

Later that night, Remy paced through her kitchen, phone tucked in her sweaty palm. She trudged into the living room, took a turn around the perimeter, then retraced her steps back into the kitchen. She opened the refrigerator, stared at the contents, closed the door and went back to pacing off her nervous energy.

The dogs joined her on her next pass. "Hey, boys, want a Milk-Bone?"

Scooby threw his head back. His version of a canine nod. Roscoe just stared up at her with round, expectant eyes.

"Come with me." She fed them each a treat, then resumed her pacing.

Her head should not be spinning like this. She should not be nervous over a phone call. What did Wyatt want to talk about? And why hadn't he called? She'd left the Latte Da hours ago. So had he. Why hadn't he contacted her yet?

For the eleventh time, she checked her phone. No new notifications. Not so much as a missed call, voice mail or unread text. Maybe her phone had a glitch. She thumbed open the screen, entered her password and then scrolled over to Wyatt's last text. We need to talk.

About what? What could be so important that couldn't wait until morning? She sank into one of the ladder-back chairs at her kitchen table and searched her mind for possible topics. The list was endless. Samson, maybe? Roscoe? World peace?

Wyatt's distinctive ringtone cut off the rest of her thoughts.

Remy's stomach clinched. She answered the call halfway through the first chorus. "Hey, Wyatt." Her voice cracked over his name.

"Did I wake you?"

"Hardly." She cleared her throat. "It's barely nine o'clock."

He went silent for several seconds. Long enough for Remy to worry he'd disconnected. "Wyatt? You still there?"

"I'm here." His tone had a tentative quality. Confusing, to say the least. He'd called her, not the other way around. What was going on with him?

She could wait him out. Except, Remy Evans waited for no man. "Want to tell me why we're talking at nine o'clock on a school night?"

"School's out for the summer, Remy."

"It was a figure of speech, Wyatt."

"Oh, right." He laughed softly. "Guess I'm a little slow on the uptake tonight."

Remy sat up straighter. "Problem with Samson?"

"He's fine. Already sound asleep."

She let out a breath. "Okay, good. Anyway… You called…because…?"

"I'm worried about you."

"Okay." That was unexpected. "Worried how?"

"I don't think you're sleeping very well."

She wasn't, but how did he know that? Was it some sort of cop instinct? Something he'd learned on the job?

"Are you still upset about Matt?"

Matt? The question had her pulling her phone down and staring at the screen. The call timer ticking under Wyatt's name said they'd been chatting less than two minutes. Huh. Shaking her head, she brought the phone back to her ear. "Truthfully? I haven't thought about him since Sunday afternoon."

"Then what's got you so upset that you can't sleep?"

You, she wanted to scream into the phone. *You're the reason I'm not sleeping.* "I didn't actually say I wasn't sleeping."

He fell silent again. Maybe he sighed. Maybe she was hearing things. "Upset, then. What's got you upset, Remy?"

"I'm not upset."

"I have a sister. I know when a woman is upset."

Oh, really? Now he definitely sounded like a cop. Or a protective big brother. Remy reined in her temper, which was, admittedly, three-quarters humiliation. "How many times do I have to tell you, Wyatt? I am *not* your sister."

"I know that." His voice held its own hint of temper. He drew in an audible breath and said in a softer, velvety tone, "Talk to me, Remy. What's going on with you? I thought we were in a good place."

"We?"

"Yes, we," he said. "We were making progress, becoming friends again. Now it's as if we've taken three steps back, and I don't like it."

She didn't, either. "I don't want to talk about this over the phone."

"Neither do I." He sounded as exasperated as she felt. "But I also don't want to let another day go by without understanding why you're pulling away from me."

"I thought *you* were pulling away from *me*."

"What? Why would I do that?" He sounded genuinely dumbfounded.

"I thought… I mean, after what I told you Sunday afternoon. You know?" She swallowed, nearly chickened out, then pressed on before she lost her nerve. "My diagnosis. I thought you…maybe, saw me differently."

"You're right. This isn't a conversation for the phone. Remy, sweetheart, I wish I could hold you right now and look you straight in the face when I tell you I don't care about the possible consequences of your endometriosis."

The gentle tone in his voice pulled tears to the very edges of her eyelashes. "Oh, Wyatt."

"Believe me when I say not in a million years could that make a difference in the way I feel about you."

"No?"

"You really haven't been paying attention, have you?" He sounded amused now. "I've been trying to ask you out on a date all week."

"You have? I…" Remy reviewed their conversations from the week. *What do you say we go out to dinner sometime?* She'd assumed he meant he wanted her to join him and Samson. "Oh, Wyatt. You really want to take me on a date?"

"I do. As soon as I can line up a babysitter for Samson."

The tears let loose then, running down her cheeks. She did her best to keep them out of her voice. "Hope and Walker's wedding is next Saturday."

He chuckled. "I know. I'm invited. But what does that have to do with our date?"

"I was thinking we could go together. You know, be each other's plus-one."

"You want us to go public in front of your entire family?" Remy wasn't sure what she heard in his voice. Surprise.

Hesitation. Maybe a combination of both? "Too much for a first date?"

"Actually—" his baritone filled her ears, the velvety tone sending a tingle down her spine "—I think that's a great idea. Let's do it, Remy. Let's go to the wedding as each other's plus-one."

She smiled through her tears. "It's a date."

Chapter Sixteen

Saturday morning dawned bright and warm, not a single cloud in the sky. Perfect weather for opening day at a petting zoo. With a million things to do before the first visitors arrived midmorning, Remy scarfed down a quick breakfast, fed the animals indoors and out, then spent the next two hours prepping her part-time staff.

Afterward, she fielded questions before dismissing them to their assigned duties.

Hands in her pockets, she watched them go. "This is going to work," she said to Scooby.

With the dog trotting along beside her, Remy walked over to the pens. Prissy ambled to the fence. "You're going to meet lots of new friends today. Can I count on you to be on your best behavior?"

The alpaca made a happy whine from deep in her throat, the sound a sort of mash-up between a lamb's baa and one of Scooby's squeaky toys.

"No spitting today," Remy warned.

Prissy just looked at her. It was the expression the alpaca often gave Wyatt. Now that he was in her mind, Remy's thoughts returned to their phone conversation. Ever since he'd asked her out, things had become easier between them. There was still tension. But a very different kind.

Anticipation, expectation. Excitement. Remy was really looking forward to their date. It was a big step, going public in front of her family.

Would one date turn to two? Three? A lifetime? She was getting ahead of herself.

The sound of gravel crunching under car tires had her consulting her watch. Ten o'clock on the dot. Her first paying customers had arrived. By noon, Grasshopper Grange pulsed with the sound of children's laughter and animal sounds. The sun washed over the duck pond in a dazzling burst of heat and light. The air held the scent of grilling hot dogs, fried dough and cotton candy. A gnawing ache twisted in Remy's stomach as she watched a young mother bouncing an infant on her lap.

She mentally shook herself before melancholy set in. Today was for enjoying her blessings, for looking ahead to what could be.

As if on cue, Wyatt's truck pulled into an empty spot in the pasture cordoned off for visitor parking. After helping Samson out of the back seat, he turned and walked straight toward Remy. No hesitation. He didn't look right or left. Just kept moving in her direction with his signature ground-eating strides. She shivered at the way his eyes held hers.

"Miss Remy!" Samson rushed ahead of his uncle and flung his arms around her waist in an all-too-brief hug. "Uncle Wyatt let me wear my Spider-Man costume, all of it, not just the top."

"It's a good look for you, kid."

"I know! Uncle Wyatt said you could paint my face again, now that he knows how to take it off. I had cereal for breakfast, but I could eat a hot dog. I'm going to miss

Puppy School, but this will be fun, too." He sucked in a breath. "Roscoe's inside, right?"

Remy managed a faint nod.

"You remembered to lock the door so no one can get in and take him?"

She managed another nod.

"Okay, good. Hey." Samson did a fast double take. "There's Toby over there with his mom."

"You better go say hello."

"No way. I'm here to work."

"Oh, you'll work." Remy ruffled his hair. "But not yet. Go play with your friend first."

"Can I, Uncle Wyatt?"

"You bet."

The boy took off.

"Slow down," Wyatt called after him. Although the warning was typical Wyatt, the words were spoken on a laugh. A change had come over the man since he'd agreed to let Remy watch his nephew that first afternoon. Wyatt was more relaxed now, and definitely less rigid. Was that because of her? She'd like to think so.

For several seconds, she watched him while he watched Samson show off his costume to his friend. Wyatt wore a pair of jeans and a light green long-sleeved T-shirt that high-lighted the color of his eyes. He'd shoved the sleeves up to his elbows, revealing his powerful forearms. He turned his head and, boom. Her heart actually went boom. "Hey," he said.

"Hey."

A slow grin spread across his face, reminding her of their kiss in his foyer. He'd been so tender with her that night, and then again on the phone last night, as if he were issuing the first of many promises.

Remy swallowed back a shiver.

"It's good to see you." Affection etched his features. "Really good."

She would have responded, if her tongue wasn't stuck to the roof of her mouth.

"Well, here I am." He spread his arms wide. "Put me to work. I'm all yours."

I'm all yours. Did he mean that the way she thought he meant it? Breathless, she got her tongue working enough to ask, "How good are you with a paintbrush?"

"If you mean, can I whitewash a fence? Not too bad."

"I mean artistically."

"Truthfully?" He scrubbed at his jaw. "About as proficient as I am at the waltz."

The words brought back an image of Wyatt dancing with the ladies at the senior center. Remy's heart pounded wildly in her chest at the memory, the pressure a slow, ruthless ache. He'd been patient with each one of his partners. He was such a decent man.

I'm all yours. Remy really hoped that was true. "I think we better play to your strengths. I'm putting you in charge of crowd control over by the duck pond."

A soft rumble of laughter sounded from his chest. "Are you expecting a riot among the feathery bunch?"

She grinned. "What can I say? With ducks, you just never know."

Confident the ducks were behaving as well as could be expected, Wyatt spent the next fifteen minutes watching Remy's part-time employee pass out individual pouches of birdseed and oats in an orderly fashion. Wyatt was superfluous. And had been from the moment he'd arrived at the edge of the pond. He was pretty sure Remy had sent him over to keep him busy. She didn't need his help.

Grasshopper Grange ran like a well-oiled machine.

Not that Wyatt was surprised. Remy was one of the most competent women he knew. Settling in to watch her work, he leaned against a tree trunk and crossed his arms over his chest. She entered the cordoned-off area with the waist-high fencing and organized thirty-plus children into a semicircle. As she put the shortest in the front, and the tallest in the back, she managed to keep the group entertained.

A succession of emotions spread through him. Awe, wonder, respect and something stronger. It was as if he'd entered some strange new dimension. The careful distance he'd kept between them since Remy had come home for good was gone. Wyatt wasn't altogether pleased.

"You're frowning. Trouble in paradise?"

Wyatt gave Reno the side-eye. "Just watching the show. And now that we're on the topic of shows—" he glared at his friend "—want to tell me why I was called out to the senior center?"

Reno threw his hands in the air. "Don't blame me for my grandmother's antics. You know Mavis. She listens to no one, sometimes not even herself."

A valid point. Also, a classic Reno evasion to a direct question. "So you had nothing to do with her little *emergency* the other night?"

"I'm wounded you would even ask." Hands back by his sides, Reno attempted to appear innocent. The man was many things. Innocent he was not. There were pictures, extensive blog posts and videos to prove it. Speaking of incriminating evidence...

"What about the video?"

"That," Reno said, chuckling, "I may have had something to do with."

"How involved were you with whole sordid affair? Out with it, Reno. Confess."

"I *may* have suggested my grandmother give you a call and I *may* have asked her to video the lesson."

"*May* have?"

"All right, all right. Truth is, I told her a video would help me learn the moves in case, you know—" he grinned "—she needed me to help her out in the future."

Classic Reno move. "I'll hand it to you," Wyatt said, shaking his head. "You got me good."

Reno laughed. "I did. I did, indeed."

"I'm honor bound to get you back, you know."

The threat only made Reno laugh harder. "Many have tried, my friend. All have failed."

None were as motivated as Wyatt. He would have engaged in more smack talk, but Remy started the show. Both men looked in her direction.

Reno had something in his gaze that didn't sit well with Wyatt. "Are you interested in Remy?"

To his credit, Reno didn't pretend to misunderstand the question. "I thought about asking her out, for maybe a hot second. But no way. I have a lot of faults. However, I have never, ever violated the bro code."

"What bro code?"

"She was always yours, Wyatt."

"She is not a commodity."

"You know that's not what I meant. Stop being stupid and make your move already." Reno waited for his words to sink in, then left Wyatt to watch the show in peace.

Happy for the solitude, Wyatt tried to pick out Samson from the assembled group of children. The boy wasn't there. He was standing just outside the enclosure next to a pony. Remy motioned Samson to bring the animal to her.

"Thank you, Samson. This is King Henry," Remy said as she stroked the animal's mane. "He's a Shetland pony. What makes him unique is his size. Shetland ponies are the smallest breed of horses. They're also very gentle and even-tempered if properly trained."

She guided the animal off to the side.

Next came a pair of lambs, once again led into the enclosure by Samson. The boy had such a look of pride on his face. Wyatt felt the same emotion move through him. "Bert and Ernie lost their mother recently, so we have to hand-feed them." She took two volunteers from the crowd and demonstrated how to give them bottles of milk.

"That's the same way my mom feeds my little sister," one of the children commented from the crowd.

"That's right." Remy's smile didn't quite reach her eyes. "It's very much the same," she said softly. She looked down for several seconds and Wyatt knew she was thinking about babies and bottles and her own diagnosis. It took great willpower not to go to her and hold her until her grief went away.

She lifted her chin. "Now for the most special animal of all."

A hush fell over the crowd.

This time, Samson led Prissy into the enclosure. Remy smiled at the boy, affection in her gaze. "Thank you, Samson. You've been a great helper this afternoon."

The boy beamed under her praise. Then, catching sight of Wyatt, trotted over. "Did you see me, Uncle Wyatt? Did you see me lead King Henry and Prissy into the viewing area?"

"I saw."

As if sensing Wyatt wasn't pleased, Samson tugged on his arm. "Did I do it wrong?"

"Not at all. You did it absolutely right."

Samson's relief was palpable. Wyatt pulled his nephew into his arms for a fast hug before the boy squirmed away.

"This is Prissy," Remy told the crowd, gaining Wyatt's attention again. "She's an alpaca and a vegetarian that likes to eat hay and grass." *And flowers*, Wyatt thought. "She also loves carrots, apples and broccoli stalks."

"She looks like a llama," someone said from the crowd of parents.

"You have a good eye," Remy said. "They're in the same family. Alpacas are smaller. Their pelts are made of superfine wool that needs shearing yearly. Alpacas are also very gentle, often timid and more relaxed than llamas. They can also learn tricks and be just plain goofy at times."

Wyatt could certainly attest to that last part.

"Why would anyone want a llama?" a little girl asked.

"Well, llamas are great, too. They can carry heavy packs all by themselves. Llamas are also very brave and trustworthy. They're natural protectors."

Samson tugged on Wyatt's arm. "You know what, Uncle Wyatt? You're just like a llama. And Miss Remy is just like an alpaca."

It was an interesting observation. The boy could be on to something. Wyatt was a protector. Remy was gentle and relaxed. They just might be each other's perfect match. Wyatt thought about their past, and all the missed opportunities. He thought about their present. More missed opportunities.

His mind turned to the future, where memories were waiting to be made. *Stop being stupid and make your move.*

Good advice. Wyatt would pull out all the stops. He would romance Remy at her brother's wedding. It probably wouldn't hurt to buy a new suit for the occasion. And maybe visit the senior center for one more dance lesson. This time he would actually pay attention. Wait, was he really considering another waltz class?

What was happening to him?

Remy was happening to him.

And Wyatt wasn't sorry about it.

Chapter Seventeen

Other than their brief encounters involving Samson, Remy didn't see much of Wyatt during the next five days. This was partially due to their work schedules, but mostly because of the events leading up to her brother's wedding. There were bridesmaids' luncheons to attend, impromptu late-night meetings to discuss a change in some detail. Then Remy's parents arrived early Wednesday morning, and things got really busy after that.

Now, Remy stood at the front of the church in her role as a bridesmaid and waited while Quinn finished her trek down the aisle ahead of the bride. Remy searched the pews for familiar faces. Or rather, one familiar face in particular. She found him immediately, in the third pew on the groom's side of the church. Wyatt held her gaze. There was a hint of a smile on his lips.

He'd come alone, just as he'd promised. *I'm getting a babysitter for Samson so this will be a real date.*

A real date. Remy clutched her bouquet tightly in her hands to keep them from shaking. Quinn took her place. The music changed. An expectant hush filled the air. The bride made her entrance. The congregation stood.

Hope came down the aisle alone.

Remy's eyes immediately filled with tears. Her future sister-in-law looked radiant in a simple, white, floor-length gown with sheer long sleeves and a fitted waistline. Hope's eyes never left Walker's. His never left hers.

She finished her journey and Brandon Stillwell, in his role as officiant, began the ceremony. "Hope and Walker—" he paused to smile at the couple "—have invited us to share in the celebration of their marriage. We come together not to mark the start of their relationship, but to recognize the bond that already exists between them…"

Remy dabbed surreptitiously at her eyes. Conflicting emotions rolled through her—joy, excitement, but also restlessness. The contradiction made her feel strangely pensive, and oddly alone. She glanced at Wyatt again and the sensation immediately dissipated. Something quite wonderful passed between them, something that stole her breath.

Biting back a sigh, she swiveled her gaze back to the bride and groom and concentrated on Walker's strong, steady voice. "I, Walker Bartholomew Evans, take thee, Hope Constance Jeffries, to be my wife. To have and to hold from this day forward, for better, for worse…"

When he finished, Hope repeated the same vows, the sound of pure love in her voice.

From her position on the church steps, Remy could see how her brother's eyes shone with the love he felt for his bride. The same look was on Hope's face. Feeling as though she was intruding on a private moment, Remy tore her gaze away. Only to find her father staring at her mother with a similar expression. After almost forty years of marriage, Lawrence and Catherine Evans were still in love.

Remy's heart lifted and she sighed at the thought. She couldn't help but wonder what it would be like to receive such a look. To be loved that well. Unable to stop herself, she glanced at Wyatt.

He was watching her.

Her world tilted on its axis.

"Marriage is a gift from God," Brandon said. "Let love rule your household. Hold fast to what is good and right and true. Outdo one another in showing mercy. And…" He paused, gave a self-deprecating laugh. "That's enough preaching from the pastor."

The congregation joined in his laughter.

Brandon finished the ceremony, then said, "It is with great honor that I declare you husband and wife. Walker, you may kiss your bride."

He gave Hope a kiss that went on entirely too long.

No one seemed to mind. Applause filled the church. The happy couple broke apart. They turned to face their family and friends. The music began again. Arm in arm, the newlyweds took off down the aisle.

Remy followed behind the others in the wedding party. She paused at Wyatt's pew long enough to say, "Meet you at the reception?"

He gave her a slow, purposeful, meaningful smile. "Your first, last and every other dance in between is mine."

Her stomach rocketed to her toes. It took tremendous concentration to continue down the aisle without tripping over her feet.

The ballroom of Thunder Ridge Country Club over-flowed with sights, sounds, and at least two hundred of the newlyweds' family and friends. Wyatt stood next to Remy, watching Walker and Hope finish their first dance as a married couple. They switched partners. Wyatt danced with his mother while Hope danced with her father.

Remy sighed. "Hope is beyond beautiful tonight. She's practically glowing with happiness."

"Don't most brides glow with happiness?"

"I certainly hope so." She glanced at him from the corner of her eye. "Quinn looks especially pretty, too."

"I hadn't noticed." Wyatt studied Remy's sister objectively. The resemblance between the women was uncanny. They had the same tilt to their pale blue eyes, the same dark hair and classic features, the same regal bearing. To Wyatt, there was no comparison. "You're much prettier."

She laughed. "Nice try, Holcomb. Everyone knows Quinn is the beauty of the family."

"Patently false and completely untrue."

"She's pregnant again. Already three months along." A host of emotions flashed in Remy's eyes. "I just found out this morning."

Wyatt contemplated what he heard in her voice. She was happy for her sister, that much was clear. But she was also sad. He knew why. "You'll be a mother one day, Remy."

"You can't know that."

"I feel it in my gut." He reached down to take her hand and laced their fingers together. The connection was light and was meant to offer her comfort. And yet, he experienced a moment of peace, a moment of rightness.

Remy meant a lot to him. He never wanted to let her go. He loved her. But Wyatt had a bad habit of failing the people he loved. Would he fail Remy, too?

Not if he worked very hard at making her happy.

He gave her hand a gentle squeeze.

She returned the gesture, then angled her head to peer into his eyes. A small, secretive smile slid across her lips. His throat seized. Remy Evans was the most beautiful woman he'd ever known.

For the rest of the night he promised himself to avoid

thinking about the future or the past. All that mattered was this moment. This night. This woman. The dance floor began filling up. The DJ played a traditional waltz next. Wyatt had paid the guy a hundred dollars to do so. "Want to dance?"

"Thought you'd never ask."

He pulled her into his arms. She shifted, settled into his embrace and off they went, their feet gliding across the parquet floor in seamless harmony. "You're very good at this," she said.

"I may have picked up a few new tricks at the senior center." Proving his expertise went beyond the basics, thanks to two more calls to the senior center for *emergencies*, and one secret trip to Mavis's dance studio, he spun Remy into a collection of complicated steps that had her gasping for air.

"Nice work, Sheriff."

"I'm a quick study."

They smiled at one another.

Wyatt changed directions, spinning Remy around the dance floor until they were both breathless. He took her through another series of spins, then slowed their pace. "Have I told you how beautiful you are tonight?"

"Several times."

"It bears repeating."

Her cheeks turned a delightful shade of pink. "You look pretty great yourself. I like the new suit."

"I bought it special for tonight."

The music stopped. By some unspoken agreement, they stayed linked in one another's arms, neither moving, neither speaking. One heartbeat passed, then another. By the third Wyatt took a deliberate step back and said, "Let's get some fresh air."

He remembered the last time they'd left a dance for

some *fresh air*. The gym had been blazing hot. He'd kissed Remy under the moon and stars. Now, like then, Wyatt guided her onto the terrace, then watched as she lifted her face to the heavens.

"What's on your mind?" he asked.

She lowered her head and gave him a smile that sent his pulse racing through his veins. "I was thinking about the last time we left a dance together. You kissed me."

"I remember."

"And then, the next day, you broke my heart."

Worst day of his high school career.

"I remember." He pulled her into his arms and simply held her against his chest, their heartbeats catching the same rhythm. "I'll never forget the look on your face. It still haunts me."

"You said the kiss meant nothing." She drew in an unsteady breath. "You said I wasn't your type."

"I lied. You were exactly my type. And the kiss?" He rested his cheek on her head. "It was everything."

"Oh, Wyatt." She pushed out of his arms. He expected to see anger on her face, not bone-deep sadness. "Why did you lie to me?"

"For a lot of reasons," he admitted.

"Give me at least one."

He gave her all of them, the same arguments her brother Casey had brought up a month ago outside Prissy's pen.

Remy shook her head. "We could have worked through all of those."

"Maybe. Maybe not," he said. "We'll never know."

"I guess we won't."

"What I *do* know," he said, reaching for her again, pulling her back into his arms, "is that we aren't kids anymore. I want to be with you, Remy. I want to explore whatever this is between us and see where it leads."

Wyatt knew where it led, to forever. But he didn't want to push her too hard, too fast. He'd hurt her once before. He didn't want to hurt her again.

"I want to be with you, too, Wyatt." She lifted her head slowly, carefully, as if she wasn't sure she believed this moment was real. "I'm also willing to see where this goes."

He kissed her then, putting his entire heart into it. The sound of voices had him setting her out of his arms. "This terrace is entirely too public. This time, I'm not giving anybody a show."

"What are you talking about, Wyatt?"

"Prom."

She gave him an odd look. "We weren't caught kissing."

"Actually," he said, "we were."

"What?" She blinked in confusion. "Someone saw us kissing?"

"I thought you knew." All this time, Wyatt had assumed Remy knew Brent had seen them kissing, and then rallied the troops to her defense. If she didn't know about that, she couldn't possibly know about her brothers' interference in their relationship. "I have to go."

"Go?" she gasped. "Go where?"

"To speak with your brother."

"Which one?"

What did it matter? They'd all overstepped. Wyatt forced himself to remember they'd done so out of love for Remy. Each had expressed legitimate concerns on her behalf. As an older brother himself, he respected their intent. He despised their methods.

Time to set things right, once and for all.

Wyatt located Brent first. "Hey, man," Brent said. "We missed you on the hiking trip last week."

"I've been busy." Wyatt swallowed. "I'm in love with Remy."

Brent's eyes widened. "That was certainly blunt and to the point."

Exasperated, Wyatt stuffed his hands in his pockets. "I'm not much for subtlety."

"Nice demonstration of that."

Wyatt frowned at his friend. "Want to take a punch at me?"

Brent pinned him with a glare, and when he spoke his voice was heavy with irony. "I'm thinking about it." As if to settle the matter, he, too, stuffed his hands in his pockets. "Does Remy know how you feel?"

"Not yet," he admitted. "I wanted to make my intentions known to her family first."

Brent arched an eyebrow. "Dude, this isn't 1873."

Wyatt ignored the dig. "Now you know where I stand. If you'll excuse me, I'm going to have this same conversation with your other brothers."

"Don't forget my father."

"Him, too." Wyatt turned to go. But pivoted back around when Brent said his name. "What?"

"Do right by my sister."

"It will be my joy and honor."

Remy tracked Wyatt through the ballroom, wondering what on earth he was doing. He made a point of speaking with each of her brothers, starting with Brent and ending with Walker. Then, he pulled her father aside for a one-on-one chat. None of the conversations lasted longer than a few minutes. A horrible, awful, wonderful thought occurred. Was he making his intentions known?

That was really kind of…sweet. And completely unnecessary. Remy was a grown woman with a mind of her own. Wyatt didn't need her family's permission to date her. Or was he asking for something more serious?

She caught up with him seconds after he walked away from her father. "What are you up to, Wyatt?"

"I was about to ask my girl to dance." He swiveled his head to the left, to the right. "You see her anywhere?"

"Ha ha. I meant with my brothers and my father. What did you say to them?"

"I was just clearing the air," he said. "Something I should have done seventeen years ago." He moved closer to her, opening his arms as if he planned to make good on the dance.

Remy stepped out of his reach. "Hold up a minute. I need to think."

"Remy, I'm not—"

"Shush." Closing her eyes, she reviewed the events of the last half hour. Wyatt kissing her, then telling her they'd been caught sneaking out of the dance back in high school. His abrupt departure, whereby he sought out all the men in her family. Finally, his revelation that he was *clearing the air* with each of them brought it all home.

This time, she was the one to say, "I have to go."

As if reading from the same script, he said, "Go? Go where?"

"To speak with my brother."

"Which one?" Wyatt asked.

"All of them." Remy left him gaping after her. She found the motley crew huddled together in the far corner of the ballroom. Whatever they were discussing, it seemed serious. Grant, Quinn's husband, was there, as well. Remy heard her name. Then Wyatt's.

She saw red. "Which one of you did it?"

All five spun around to look at her. Casey spoke for the group. "Did what?"

Remy jammed her hands on her hips. "Who read Wyatt the riot act after he kissed me at the prom?"

Five gazes immediately dropped to the ground. No one spoke. But there was a lot of avoiding direct eye contact. Approaching the most likely candidate, Remy pointed a finger at Brent. "It was you, wasn't it?"

"You better believe I said something to Wyatt." He lifted his chin at an unrepentant angle. "You were barely fifteen. He was practically eighteen, with one foot already out of town on a fancy football scholarship. So, yeah, I told him to back off."

"I said something to him, too," Casey admitted. "No one messes with my little sister."

"You actually said that to him?"

"Pretty much." There wasn't an ounce of remorse in her brother's tone. "Now that you've heard our true confessions, you might as well know. Brent and I weren't the only ones who confronted Wyatt."

McCoy and Walker declared their guilt next, one right after the other.

The mortifying revelations just keep coming, Remy thought, blinking at her brothers in cold, quiet shock. She decided it couldn't get any worse. But then, Grant dug the knife in deeper. "I said something, too."

"Are you kidding me right now?" Her fists clenched by her sides. "You were only dating my sister at the time."

"I was working up the nerve to ask her to marry me. But, yeah. What Casey said." Grant lifted his chin now. "No one messes with my little sister."

Remy was too angry to cry. She was actually too angry to speak. This universal show of support should have given her the warm fuzzies. All she felt was complete and utter humiliation. No wonder Wyatt had dumped her like a hot potato.

There were times she was proud to be an Evans. This was not one of them.

A hand closed gently over her arm. "Remy."

"Not now, Wyatt."

"Remy," he said again, more firmly. "Come on, it's okay." He took hold of her shoulders and turned her around to face him. "It's all in the past."

"But they—"

"Were protecting their little sister."

"Yeah, but they…" Shaking her head, she glanced over her shoulder. Her brothers were still there, wearing duplicate expressions of remorse. And then, they started speaking at once.

They were sorry. They didn't mean to hurt her. They meant well. Their hearts were in the right place. Yada, yada, yada. All probably true.

Still, Remy wasn't ready to forgive them. She would, eventually. Once the shock and horror wore off. In the meantime, she turned back to Wyatt. His tender smile washed away the worst of her anger. "I'd like that dance now," she said in a shamefully weak voice.

"You got it."

She stepped into his waiting arms and let him whisk her away.

Chapter Eighteen

Wyatt began the week with sisters on his mind, and the things brothers did to protect them. The choices weren't always easy. Mistakes were often made. Some of which left permanent scars. What Remy's brothers did seventeen years ago was forgivable. In fact, looked at from a certain angle, their behavior could even be considered noble.

His mind went to his own sister. He needed to see CiCi, and so he applied for visitation. Once the approval came through, he would make the fifty-minute drive to her prison in Denver.

In the meantime, Wyatt focused on hiring the new deputy. He'd narrowed the field down to two candidates. Now, as he reviewed his notes from both the phone calls and subsequent in-person interviews, one candidate in particular stood out. A police detective currently working for the Denver PD. The woman had an interesting past. She'd been a professional snowboarder before becoming a cop. She also knew Reno. From her unsolicited comments, it was clear she wasn't a fan of the "Bad Boy of the Slopes." There was a story there, but Wyatt hadn't asked for details. Bottom line, Detective Phoebe Foxe was the right person for the job.

He opened his email and sent the offer letter. While he typed, the approval for his prison visit with CiCi came through. After informing Doris of his hiring decision, he said, "I'm heading to the Denver Women's Correctional Facility."

For once, Doris didn't demand an explanation or ask when she could expect his return. She was too busy dancing at her desk over his choice of candidates. It would take a long time for Wyatt to get that particular image out of his head.

He arrived in plenty of time for processing at Denver's Women's Correctional Facility. Mindful of the strict dress code, he'd changed out of his uniform into a pair of worn jeans and a basic navy blue T-shirt. He filled out the necessary paperwork, produced his driver's license and was immediately led into the visitation area.

He'd done a lot of thinking on the drive and realized how much he'd changed since spending time with Remy. Now, as he waited for CiCi to be brought in, Wyatt made himself three promises. First, he was going to let up on the restrictions he'd placed on Samson. Not all of them, but he was going to give the boy room to explore his artistic side.

Next, he was going to let the boy bring his puppy home. Lastly, Wyatt was going to tell Remy he loved her. He was mentally rehearsing his speech when the door on his right swung open. Prisoners in orange jumpsuits moved into the room, single file. CiCi was third in line.

Wyatt rose to his feet and studied his sister shuffling in his direction. No one would doubt they were related. They had the same eye color. The same lean build with long runner's legs and defined muscles in their arms. CiCi's hair was several shades lighter than Wyatt's, strawberry blond to his dark auburn, and she was definitely more feminine.

It was good to see her.

Per the rules, they were permitted to embrace at the beginning and end of each visit. Wyatt pulled his sister into a hug. The sudden ache in his heart was love. She was his family, his blood. She'd made terrible choices, but that didn't change how he felt about her.

Setting her out of his arms, he gestured for her to sit at the small table he'd commandeered for their visit. Eyes not quite meeting his, she did as he directed. She looked so small, so lost and vulnerable. "It's good to see you, CiCi."

She looked at him without actually making eye contact. "Hi, Wyatt."

Hi, Wyatt. Not *good to see you.* Not *I've missed you.* He ignored the pain of her subtle rejection. Clearly, she still held him responsible for her incarceration. He *was* responsible. As the arresting officer, he'd started the ball rolling.

CiCi had left him with no other option. She had to know that. Wyatt had given her chance after chance until his trust was eroded into doubt and suspicion. His decision to haul her to jail had been more about protection than punishment. The prison had put her in a treatment program. Her incarceration kept her clean. No more access to drugs, alcohol or pills.

Then why didn't she look healthier? Why did she still look so beaten down? Discouragement swamped him. "Are they treating you well?"

Her head bobbed up and down.

"You'd tell me if they weren't?"

More head bobbing.

He reached over and took her hand, tapping into the same unruffled calm he'd used when Samson suffered a nightmare. "Tell me what's going on, CiCi. I can see something's bothering you." Her composure was fragile at best. "You can tell me anything."

"I'm fine." Deliberately, and with considerable care, she

pulled her hand free. Point taken. She didn't want him to touch her. Time, he told himself. It would take time for CiCi to understand why he'd arrested her.

For now, Wyatt steered the conversation along a different path. "Samson is showing a lot of artistic talent." He told CiCi about the series of blueprints for his dream day care. "He was really paying attention during all those home improvement shows he watched with you."

She flinched. "You mean the ones I *made* him watch instead of cartoons because the music got on my nerves?"

"In many ways you've been a good influence on your son, CiCi. Don't ever doubt that."

Her face turned ashen at his words. "Not good enough."

"That's all in the past," he said. "It's a new day."

She pinned him with a glare at odds with her defeated body language. "I failed my son." Her voice was heavy with self-condemnation. "I put my own needs ahead of his. Nothing I do will ever change that."

"It's in the past," he said again. "You made mistakes, yes. But Samson is only seven. The resiliency of youth is on his side. And yours, CiCi. You're still young. It's not too late to start over."

Her head lowered. "I hate what I did to my little boy. I left him alone, a lot, not just the night he called you. There's no coming back from that, Wyatt. There is no atonement."

"That's not true. God's purpose for you is bigger than your mistakes."

She refused to look at him.

"You're not alone, CiCi. I'm on your side. You won't have to start over by yourself. I'll be with you every step of the way."

His words produced another long, unresponsive silence. "I can't do it," she whispered. "I'm not strong enough."

"I'll be strong for both of us."

"You just don't get it, Wyatt." She let out a choked, piti-ful sob. "I was never meant to be a mother. I don't *want* to be a mother. It's too hard."

Outraged on Samson's behalf, Wyatt forced himself to remember CiCi had been sober for seven months, and not by choice. She was still in the early stages of recovery.

As he stared at his sister's wide, frightened eyes, Wyatt was reminded of what Brandon once said in a sermon. We don't mature at the top of the mountain but during the climb. CiCi was still on the ascent.

"…And that's why I want you to contact your attorney."

Wyatt pinched the bridge of his nose, trying to focus on what she'd just asked of him, praying he'd heard wrong. "Tell me again why you want me to contact Mitch."

"I want to give you full custody of Samson." She lifted her chin and tried to sound matter-of-fact. She failed mis-erably.

"You don't mean that."

"I do mean it." CiCi gave him a clear-eyed stare, not frightened, not hesitant. Determined. "I don't want to be Samson's mother anymore."

She stood then.

Scrambling to his feet, Wyatt reached to her. "CiCi, wait. Don't—"

"Make it happen, Wyatt." With abnormal calm, she left him staring after her, his hand outstretched, his heart ach-ing. For her. For Samson.

For all of them.

Per Wyatt's request in a series of brief texts, Remy drove Samson home from her nieces' sixth birthday party. "Did you have a good time today?"

"Yeah, I guess so. It was fun." She could practically hear his caveat: *For a girl's party.*

She tried not to laugh. "What was the best part?"

"The waterslide."

Remy had already guessed he'd say that. She'd had to drag the boy away when it was time to eat and open presents, and again when it was time to leave.

"You know what, Miss Remy?" He grinned at her with that light in his eye that foreshadowed a spurt of creativity. "I'm going to add a waterslide to my day care as soon as I get home."

She'd figured he'd say that, as well. "I think that's a brilliant idea."

They arrived at Wyatt's house with Samson's running commentary on what kind of slide he was going to design, how big it would be, plus countless other details. To Remy's surprise, Wyatt's truck sat in the drive. She hadn't expected him back from Denver until well after six. Had something happened during his visit with CiCi?

Using the key Wyatt had loaned her earlier in the week, she let herself and Samson into the darkened foyer. True to his word, the little boy rushed ahead of her and went straight up the stairs, presumably to begin work on his latest set of blueprints.

Remy moved deeper into the house. The completely dark, silent, *empty* house. "Wyatt?"

She turned on lights, called out again. Still no sign of the man. After a full circuit of the first floor, she eventually found him sitting on the back stoop. He stared at the woods beyond his property line, elbows resting on his knees.

Something about his manner told her he was upset. She sat beside him. "Hey."

He continued looking out into the distance. "Where's Samson?"

"Upstairs, adding a waterslide to his day care." She gave a soft laugh. "I predict it will look much like the one at the party today, but with several upgrades."

Wyatt drew in a hard breath. "I love that kid."

Remy did, too, as much as if he were her own son. She'd fallen hard for the boy, almost as hard as she'd fallen for his uncle. Her love for both would last longer than a lifetime. She nearly confessed her feelings right there on the spot. But something was off with Wyatt. Something that had put him in a brooding mood. He never brooded. "How did the visit go with your sister?"

"Not great."

His voice was lousy with sorrow. But it was the look in his eyes that had her throat burning. Devastation, worry, a big brother unable to help his little sister no matter how hard he tried. "How bad was it?"

"CiCi wants to give me permanent custody of Samson." Wyatt turned his head and leveled stricken eyes on her face. "She doesn't want to be his mother anymore."

Remy heard Wyatt's words, but she was too numb to feel anything beyond soul-deep agony. This was all too terrible and gut-wrenching to be real. "Oh, Wyatt." She fought to keep her voice even. "CiCi loves Samson. I know she does. How could she not? He's a great kid. She couldn't possibly want to give him away."

He swung his gaze back to the woods. "Difficult to know for sure."

Hardly able to breathe, she touched his arm. "Tell me everything she said."

He laid it all out for her, from the moment he sat at the table in the prison to when CiCi asked him to get in touch with his attorney. "And then, after telling me she didn't want to be Samson's mother anymore, she just stood up, said, 'Make it happen, Wyatt,' and walked away."

Sharp pain arrowed through Remy's heart. She had never seen Wyatt wear such an expression, one of dazed misery. Poor Wyatt. *Poor Samson.* She prayed the little boy never found out what his mother said today. "You aren't angry at CiCi?"

"Oh, I'm angry." He swiped the back of his hand across his mouth. "But I also believe she'll change her mind once she's had more time to think."

"I pray you're right."

"But if she doesn't…" Wyatt laced their fingers together. "We'll deal with it together."

We. Together. The promise wasn't just in the words, but in the way he held on to her hand. "Yes," she said, squeezing gently. "We will deal with it together. In the meantime, why don't we take a look at the latest addition Samson has added to his day care."

Wyatt's smile almost reached his eyes. "Best suggestion I've heard all day. But before we go inside, I need to thank you."

"For what?"

"For being you." He pressed his lips to hers in a brief, fast, sweet kiss, the move as natural as breathing. "I have more to say, but not now. Later."

"I have things to say to you, as well."

They entered the house. Wyatt moved to the bottom of the stairs. "Samson?" he called out. "Samson, you still up there?" He waited several beats. "Samson?"

"Maybe he's so focused on the plans he didn't hear you," Remy suggested.

"Maybe." Wyatt mounted the first step, then went unnaturally still. "Something doesn't feel right. Do me a favor, check in the garage and see if his bike is in there."

"You don't think he went bike riding without your permission?"

"I don't know what I think." He took the stairs two at a time.

Remy ran to the garage. In her haste, she nearly tripped over the storage tube she'd bought for Samson. She absently picked it up and rushed into the garage. Samson's bike was gone. *Please, Lord, no...*

Setting the storage tube down in the foyer, she rushed to the foot of the stairs. "Wyatt. Is he up there?"

"No. Is he down there?"

"No, but his bike is gone."

A muffled response joined the sound of footsteps pounding down the stairs. They stood side by side, staring at each other for three long seconds.

"Do you think he overheard our conversation about his mother?" she asked.

"Possibly."

They shared a horrified glance, then ran out the door side by side. They searched the front yard. The backyard. The garage once more. "His bike is definitely gone," Wyatt said. "No telling where he went."

Tamping down her terror, Remy looked to the sky. The sun would set soon. Night would come next. Remy's lips parted in a silent cry. But then, calm set in. "I know where he is."

"How can you?"

She'd never been more certain of anything in her life. "I just know."

Wyatt tried, without success, to smother the blast of panic that surged through him. Samson was out there—somewhere—alone. If he was taken by a stranger, or had fallen off his bike, or was hurt in any other way—

No, he couldn't let his mind go down that road. He was a cop. He knew what to do when a child went missing. He let his training kick in and reached for his phone.

"What are you doing?" Remy asked.

My job. "Organizing a search party."

"I don't think that's necessary. I know where he is."

Her words threatened to destroy what little control Wyatt had left. "There's no possible way you can know where my nephew went."

"Don't dismiss me, Wyatt. I've spent a lot of time with Samson. I know how he thinks."

Wyatt looked away from Remy, battling for calm, hearing the seconds tick off in his head as if each was a gunshot. "One month does not make you an expert on my nephew."

"I'll ignore your insult because I know you're upset." Her voice was low and strained and very, very insistent. "But it's a mistake to assume I don't know what's going on in Samson's head right now. All you have to do is look at the drawings of your nephew's dream day care to know where he went."

"You expect me to trust you on something this important?"

"Yes, Wyatt." She held his gaze. "That's exactly what I expect."

The sight of her, proud and strong and confident, threatened to destroy what little composure he had left. He wanted to believe her. But if she was wrong, Samson would be the one to pay the price. "I'm sorry, Remy. I can't."

"Can't," she repeated, her voice devoid of emotion. "Or won't?"

He knew what he said next could define their relationship. It could possibly even destroy any chance of a future together. He had to take that chance. Samson's life depended on Wyatt thinking like a cop. "We're wasting time arguing about this."

He charged back into the house, grabbed his keys and did his best not to think about the look of disappointment on Remy's face. The sound of her car starting up told its own story. Wyatt would explain himself later.

Right now, Samson was his priority. First order of business, he had to contact his deputy on duty. He was thumbing open his phone when the blue storage tube caught his eye. *All you have to do is look at the drawings of your nephew's dream day care to know where he went.*

Was Remy right? He twisted open the tube and pulled out the thick roll of papers. Samson had numbered and dated each page. Wyatt quickly flipped through the stack and immediately began to understand his nephew better. Each of Samson's drawings represented a sense of fun but with a heavy respect for order. The boy had an amazing imagination, but he also appreciated organization and symmetry.

Wyatt had been so busy trying to keep Samson safe and out of trouble he'd missed the boy's very essence. Wyatt took another pass through the drawings. It was the second time through that helped him realize why Remy was so certain she knew where Samson had gone. Although each drawing was vastly different from the next, there was always one addition that never varied. Samson had labeled the room Doggie Day Care.

Wyatt's phone dinged with an incoming text. He checked the screen. Remy had sent a picture. Samson sitting on her porch steps, head bent, a familiar puppy on his lap.

Wyatt texted back while running to his truck. On my way.

Chapter Nineteen

Remy sat next to Samson, heart pounding, breath clogging in her throat. The boy hadn't spoken since she'd put Roscoe on his lap. When she'd first come upon him, he'd looked so pitiful, desperately trying not to cry. She'd considered taking him back to his uncle. But had abandoned the idea as soon as Samson begged to see his puppy one last time.

"One last time?" she'd asked.

"Before I run away for good and never, ever come back." His control shattered then, and he broke down into gut-wrenching sobs.

Remy had held the little boy close until his anguish gave way to shuddering gulps of air. "Okay. Okay. Sit down, Samson." She pointed to the stairs leading up to her front porch. "I'm going to get Roscoe now."

She'd retrieved the puppy, sent a quick picture to Wyatt, then sat down on the step beside Samson. Tears still tracked down the little boy's cheeks. "Do you have a place picked out where you plan to go?" she asked.

"Anywhere my mom can't find me. Not that she'd come looking." He buried his face into Roscoe's neck. "She hates me."

If Remy had wondered how much Samson had heard

of her conversation with Wyatt, she had her answer now. He'd heard too much. "Your mother doesn't hate you." Remy refused to believe otherwise.

"Then why doesn't she want to be my mom anymore?"

Remy thought hard before responding. She hadn't been at the prison, but she knew enough to say, "Your mom was having a bad day. I'm sure she didn't mean it."

Samson lifted his head. "You really think so?"

The hope Remy heard in the little boy's voice severed her heart with the precision of a steel blade. "You are the most special little boy I know. Any woman would be proud to call you her son."

"Would you?"

She was undone. Completely, forever lost to this little boy. "I definitely would. I love you, Samson." She roped her arm around his shoulders and tugged him up against her. "So very, very much."

"Do you love me as much as you love Scooby and Prissy?"

"A thousand times more."

"I love you, too." He started crying again.

Remy did, too. Just then, Wyatt's truck came wheeling around the corner and screeched to a gravel-kicking halt. He flew out of the vehicle and ran to them, the door swinging on its hinges. Seeing their faces, he ground to a halt.

"There you are." The lightness of his tone belied the fear swirling in his eyes. "I thought I lost you both."

Remy's heart gave a few thick, hard beats. "We're still here."

Her words caused a quick indrawn pull of air. "No thanks to me," he muttered under his breath. "Can I join you?"

Remy looked at Samson. He nodded, then they both scooted over so that Wyatt could fit on the step beside them. "We were just talking about Samson's mother."

Remy caught Wyatt's eye over the boy's head. "And how much she loves him despite what she said today."

Wyatt took his cue. "It's true, Samson. Your mother loves you very much."

"You said she doesn't want me anymore."

Wyatt winced. "I'm sorry you had to hear that. Your mother was having a bad day. She'll change her mind once she feels better."

"That's what Miss Remy said."

"Miss Remy is very wise." Wyatt looked at her again, his eyes full of apology. "We would both be smart to listen to her."

The little boy fell silent, as if considering this.

"You can always count on me to take care of you, Samson," Wyatt said. "I love you. I have since the day you were born. And, because I love you, I've decided to ease up on some of the rules in our house. Not all of them," he clarified. "But one in particular. Roscoe can come live with us at our house."

The transformation in Samson was nothing short of remarkable. "You really mean it?"

"I really mean it."

"I love you, Uncle Wyatt."

Wyatt laughed, ruffled the boy's hair in the way Remy often did. "That's good to hear."

Holding Roscoe close, Samson sprang from the step. "Can I go tell Scooby and Farrell the good news?"

"By all means."

The boy ran into the house, shouting the dog's name, and then the ferret's.

Wyatt stared after his nephew, his gaze troubled. "I'm not naive enough to think one conversation will make all this go away. Or fix the damage I inadvertently did to the boy." He swung back around to face Remy. "Samson and I start counseling next week."

"I think that's a wonderful idea."

Eyes locked with hers, he gained his feet, tugging her up with him. "I also hurt you and I'm sorry."

"About…?"

"The way I behaved this afternoon." He cupped her hand between his. "I dismissed you and your insight into my nephew. I ignored your wisdom in favor of police procedure."

No man had ever spoken to her with such remorse in his tone, or sincerity in his eyes. But Wyatt's dismissal had really cut deep. "Keep talking."

"My greatest offense was to put my fear ahead of my trust in you."

It took a special person to admit when he was wrong. Was it any wonder she loved this man? "Anything else?"

"I'm an idiot."

"I wouldn't go that far…"

"I'll never second-guess you again, Remy. Can you forgive me?"

"Of course I forgive you." She glanced down at their joined hands. "I love you, Wyatt. With all that I am."

"I love you, too, Remy." He pulled her to him. "I've loved you since I was seventeen. I will love you until the day I die."

"Oh, Wyatt." She lifted onto her toes and kissed him. "I love you now, forever and beyond."

"We have a lot of lost time to make up for. I don't want to squander another minute. Remy Evans?" Still holding her hand, he lowered to one knee. "Will you marry me?"

"Yes. Oh, yes, Wyatt. Absolutely yes. And…um… Don't make any sudden moves." She tugged him to his feet. "We have an audience."

His eyes filled with amusement. "Let me guess. Prissy is out of her pen again."

"And standing right behind you."

Wyatt pivoted slowly around and opened his arms wide. "Come on, girlfriend. Hit me with your best shot."

The alpaca shuffled to her left. Shifted back to her right. Took two steps forward. Then paused, blinked and nuzzled Wyatt's cheek, as if to say, *Welcome to the family.*

Remy couldn't think of a better way to start the rest of their lives.

Epilogue

One year later

After considerable debate, Remy and Wyatt chose to hold the party at Wildlife World. Their special day required a special venue. They'd closed the zoo two hours early for the event.

"It's been a memorable year," Quinn said, hooking her arm through Remy's as they stood on the gazebo overlooking a large meadow filled with family and friends.

"One for the record books," Remy agreed.

It was no small exaggeration. Wyatt had insisted on a short engagement. They'd married a week before the new school year began, which had been two weeks after Remy secured her loan to purchase Wildlife World from her neighbors.

Samson had served as Wyatt's best man. The boy had been beyond excited when they'd told him they were all three moving into Remy's house after the wedding. CiCi hadn't changed her mind about giving over custody to Wyatt, but she hadn't signed any papers yet. Whatever her ultimate decision, Samson would always have a home with

Remy and Wyatt. For now, they took one day at a time, knowing each was a blessing straight from God.

Days after the Christmas holidays were over, Quinn and her husband welcomed a healthy baby boy into their family. Hope had given birth to a girl four months later.

And then, Remy and Wyatt had beaten the odds. "We've had a lot to celebrate as a family," she said to her sister.

Quinn's eyes dropped to Remy's protruding midsection. "With more blessings on the way."

They shared a smile, then both looked out over the assembled group. Quinn's eight-year-old daughters were teaching Harper and Kennedy how to play croquet. Samson and his friend Toby were engaged in a classic game of tag, with Scooby and Roscoe unsure of the rules but having a ball following hard on the little boys' heels. Walker and Grant were on baby duty, both looking like the proud papas they were.

Wyatt hustled up the gazebo steps, carrying an enormous black balloon covered with question marks. "I need to borrow my wife."

"She's all yours." Quinn stepped away from Remy.

"You ready for this, Mrs. Holcomb?"

"More than ready."

Wyatt handed over the balloon, then reached for the equally enormous stick pin he'd placed on the banister before their guests started arriving. "You want to do the honors, or should I?"

"I was thinking we'd let Samson." Remy covered her round belly with her hand.

"Okay." Wyatt kissed her hard on the lips. "Be right back." He corralled Samson, then called everyone over to the gazebo for the gender reveal of their unborn baby.

Quinn moved in beside Remy again. "Brace yourself, little sister. You're about to receive a pretty big surprise."

She shot the other woman a confused stare.

"Just wait," Quinn said, looking curiously smug.

Because Remy and Wyatt wanted to find out the gender of their baby at the same time as everyone else, they'd given Quinn the sealed envelope from the doctor and asked if she would tell the florist what color confetti to put inside the balloon. Quinn had been thrilled and had told them both, "Your secret is safe with me."

Samson and Wyatt returned, with the rest of their guests gathering around expectantly. Samson was too excited to stand still. "I can't wait to burst the balloon."

Remy gave him the pin. "Go for it."

There was a loud pop and then confetti rained down. Not blue, not pink, but a collection of both. What kind of trick was Quinn playing? Remy glared at her sister, who was grinning like a loon.

"Surprise!" Quinn said, throwing her hands up in the air. "You're having twins."

"Twins?"

"One boy, one girl."

Remy's legs buckled under her. Wyatt was instantly by her side. "Twins?" she whispered. "We're having twins."

Wyatt whooped. "Did you hear that?" he shouted to the equally confused crowd. "Remy and I are having twins! A boy *and* a girl."

There was a lot of hooting and hollering after that.

Laughing, Samson fell to the ground and made a snow angle in the multicolored confetti. Remy smiled up at her husband. "Twins, Wyatt!"

"Two for the price of one." He gave her a long, sweet kiss. "I love you, Remy."

"I love you more."

"Nope." He pressed his lips to her temple, her cheek, her nose. "Not possible."

"Well," she said, "I've certainly loved you longer."

"Again, no. Give it up, Mrs. Holcomb. This is the one argument, perhaps the only argument in our marriage, you will never win."

It was also the only argument she never got tired of losing.

* * * * *

*If you loved this story,
check out the previous book
in the Thunder Ridge series by Renee Ryan*

Surprise Christmas Family

And be sure to check out these other great books

A Plan for Her Future *by Lois Richer*
The Texan's Truth *by Jolene Navarro*
Seeking Sanctuary *by Susanne Dietze*

Available now from Love Inspired!

Find more great reads at www.LoveInspired.com

Dear Reader,

I love animals. They have a way of softening hearts and teaching us unconditional love. For that, and many other reasons, I never grow tired of adding four-legged characters to my books, often in the form of dogs and puppies.

It wasn't until Prissy sashayed onto the page (and past Wyatt's window) that I found myself writing entire scenes with an animal actually stealing the show. As creative as she was at finding ways out of her pen, Prissy was even better at wrestling the spotlight from the other characters. I truly fell in love with her. She is one of my favorite secondary characters. If you want to see her sweet perma-grin close up, I have pictures of her on my website and social media pages.

I'm also a fan of home renovation shows. There's something about watching an ordinary room transform into a spectacular space that makes me feel both happy and inspired. How easy it would have been to give my heroine this same passion. Just like her alpaca, Remy proved difficult. She had zero interest in remodeling her home, discussing backsplashes or looking at paint swatches. Samson, on the other hand, came through for me. The little boy couldn't stop redesigning his day care. Well, when he wasn't playing with puppies or riding his bike, that is. Kid after my own heart.

I hope you enjoyed hanging out in my fictional Colorado town as much as I did. While this was my second trip to Thunder Ridge, it won't be my last. More stories coming soon.

In the meantime, I love hearing from readers. Feel free to stop by my website, www.reneeryan.com. You can also contact me by email at ReneeRyanBooks@gmail.com, or on my Renee Ryan Facebook page. My Twitter handle is @reneeryanbooks.

Happy Reading!
Renee

WE HOPE YOU ENJOYED
THIS BOOK FROM

LOVE INSPIRED
INSPIRATIONAL ROMANCE

Uplifting stories of faith, forgiveness and hope.

Fall in love with stories where faith helps
guide you through life's challenges, and discover
the promise of a new beginning.

6 NEW BOOKS AVAILABLE EVERY MONTH!